GATORS

STEVE R. YEAGER

SEVERED PRESS
HOBART TASMANIA

GATORS

ALSO BY STEVE R. YEAGER

Raptor Apocalypse

Red Asphalt: Raptor Apocalypse Book 2

Righteous Apostate: Raptor Apocalypse Book 3

Zombie Team Alpha

AUTHOR'S NOTE

I started working on Gator before the terrible incident at Disneyland in Florida occurred. The impetus for this tale was a previous news story about a giant alligator being spotted running wild on a Florida golf course. At one point, I almost ceased work on this book due to the nature of the toddler's death, but I also believe that this story is different enough from that tragedy and still deserves to be told.
I hope you enjoy it.

ONE

SLICED IT

"WOULD YOU HURRY it the hell up?" McGee said, leaning heavily on his Callaway Big Bertha driver.

"Hold your damn horses, will ya? You can't rush a pro." Harold Robertson set his feet and wound up into his backswing.

He tended to bend his left arm on occasion, so tonight he was working hard at keeping it straight, just as that one-fifty-per-hour instructor had told him to do. There was real money on the line today. A hundred bucks a stroke to the winner of the round, and he was down by ten strokes already.

He snap-pivoted and swung.

And missed the ball.

McGee, Johnson, and Little Lord Fauntleroy—as he was known by those who preferred to mock him—collapsed in hysterical laughter.

"You can't hit for shit," Johnson chided, stopping his chuckling long enough to speak. "Maybe you need another drink."

"Yeah," McGee added. He tossed a bottle of Macallan 25 at Harold, who had to drop his oversized driver to catch it.

"You sure can catch better than you can swing, that's for damn sure," Johnson said.

"And he...and he..." said Fauntleroy, whose real name was just 'Roy.' They teased him incessantly because he spoke so funny

1

and his hair was a mop of blond. If you didn't know the guy, you'd think it was a wig, or some kind of dead animal lying atop his head.

Harold uncorked the bottle and took a long pull. After plugging the cork back in, he pinched the bottle between his thighs and wiggled it back and forth like it was a big, swinging dick.

"You wish," McGee said. "Keep dangling it out there like that and some gator's gonna come'n bite it off."

"That'd still leave it longer than your tiny pecker," Harold said.

"That so...? Okay, then." McGee raised an eyebrow as he nodded. "Now that you've had a little fortification, let's get this sideshow going, right ladies? Sun's already going down. Gonna be dark soon, and we still got two more holes left to get to. Don't wanna go chasing my balls once it gets dark."

"No one does," Johnson quipped.

The entire group again broke out in laughter. Harold Robertson set the bottle down and picked up his club. He adjusted his belt and pulled his shorts out of the crack in his ass and again hovered over his ball. This time, he wasn't going to miss. If he did, that would make it two whiffs in a row. Double choke. He'd never live it down, and the whole thing would end up costing him a day's pay, maybe more. While he could afford the cost, it was the constant badgering by his friends he wanted to avoid.

"Hurry the hell up," McGee chided, picking up the bottle.

"Yeah, I heard you the first time. Just shut yer damn mouth, K?" Harold wiped the beading sweat from his eyebrows, stuck his butt out, and wriggled it back and forth while setting his feet. He checked his swing and watched the club head, then drew back and swung for all he was worth.

And sliced it.

Gah! He'd bent his damn arm again. The ball made a buzzing noise as it spun off to the left. It cleared a hanging dogwood tree and disappeared into the swampy marsh far outside the rough.

"*Dammit!*" he yelled.

Fresh laughter broke out all around.

Harold wrenched his hands on the club. He wanted to throw it to the ground, but didn't. Then he caught himself a hair short of raising the damn thing and snapping it in two across his thigh. But he'd catch even more flak for doing that. *Just breathe*, he told himself. *Don't want to die of a heart attack.*

"O—kay," McGee said, still chuckling. "Let's jus' get going. Daylight's burning, ladies. Bugs'll be eating us alive soon, and I just want to be done and collect my winnings. Forget the damn ball, Harry. Since you are such a lousy golfer, we'll let you drop outside the green. For an additional C-note, that is."

"No," Harold said. "I'm gonna find my goddamned ball if it takes me all night."

McGee uncorked the bottle and took a swig, then wiped the dribbling brown liquid off his chin with the back of his hand. "Suit yourself, ya damn fool. Just watch out for gators, hear? They been harassing good folk lately. Wouldn't want that big 'ole pecker of yours to go missing."

Again, the three men laughed. Harold didn't.

TWO

FAMILY DINNER

NEWLY HIRED FLORIDA sheriff's deputy, Travis Morrison, hefted a spoonful of mashed potatoes onto his plate. He smiled at his son beside him and his wife directly across the table from him. Then he folded his hands together and said a quick prayer of thanks to the man upstairs.

The thanks was for his family and not at all for the steaming pile of shit he'd stepped in moving them to such a remote armpit of a town, so near a soggy, fetid swamp. What the hell had he been thinking when he had accepted the damn job? He hadn't been thinking, that's what. But it was only for a year. Just long enough to get back on his feet—after the shooting.

"How was your day?" he asked his son Jeremy.

His son said nothing.

"Your father asked you a question," said Colleen from across the table as she served herself a helping of steaming broccoli from a stoneware dish.

Jeremy dug at the potatoes on his plate, raking his fork back and forth across the top of them and making fine groves in the starchy surface. Travis scoffed at him then cut into his steak and bent sideways to check it. Rare, just how he liked it. Even in the completely different climate from his home state of Oregon, his wife could cook like a pro. That's partly why he married her. The other part was that she was honest to a T—and loyal, and smarter than him by a mile. She'd proven it all ten times over when she'd stuck by him after the terrible mistake he'd made shooting that kid.

Jeremy continued to play with his food, but would not touch it.

"You want something else?" Colleen asked her son.

Travis grunted his disapproval.

"He has to eat something," she said.

Travis raised his fork and pointed at his boy. "If he's hungry enough, he'll eat." There was a hint of anger in his voice.

"Hey," Colleen said, "go easy on him."

"I'm just saying he'll eat when he's good and hungry, that's all."

Almost a minute passed in near silence. The only noises came from the clinking of forks and knives and the soft squishy chewing sounds Travis made as he worked on his steak. The clock on the wall behind Colleen ticked, and the minute hand lurched forward.

Jeremy still hadn't taken a bite of his dinner.

"Eat," Travis said, stabbing his fork toward his son's dinner plate. He took a drink of ice water and flung the glass's dewy condensation on the floor. Everything was so damn humid here. You could almost cut it with a knife. The unrelenting heat required he shower twice a day, minimum, and an hour after showering he'd be drenched in sticky sweat again. Like a damn sauna.

Jeremy sat back in his chair and folded his arms defensively over his chest.

Shaking his head, Travis glanced at his wife. She sighed as she nibbled on a crown of broccoli.

"At least eat your vegetables, dear," she said.

Jeremy pushed himself back from the table. "I *hate* it here! I hate it!"

Travis pointed with his fork. "That talk's not acceptable at the dinner table. Hate it here or not, it's where we are now. So you'd better get used to it." He lowered his fork, realizing he was lecturing himself just as much as he was his son. He glanced down at his plate.

"Did something happen at school today?" Colleen asked.

"No, Mom. I just hate this place so much. The bugs, the snakes, the people, alligators...*everything!*"

Travis looked up and slightly raised his hand, but before he could speak, his wife beat him to the punch.

"Your father has worked very hard to get us here. You should appreciate the sacrifices he makes and all that he does for us. He even got you into the best middle school they have in the whole area." She shook her head. "He's even scheduled his work hours just so he can drop you off every morning. Don't you think you should be more appreciative of that?"

"No," Jeremy said. He got up from the table and stormed off, saying with his back turned, "I don't want to live here. And *nobody* wants us living here, either!"

Colleen started to rise from her chair, but Travis put a hand on her forearm to stop her.

"Guess he hates it here," she said, shrugging. One corner of her mouth ticked up as she grinned crookedly back at him.

Travis swallowed. "I know."

"But it is only for a year still, right?"

"Hopefully."

"Then we'll just have to make it work." She reached across the table and patted the back of his hand.

He lifted his hand and put it on top of hers. "You are too good for me."

"And you'd better not damn well forget it."

He laughed and squeezed her hand. "Like you would ever let me forget."

"Dang straight," she said, giving a single nod.

They both resumed eating. Another minute passed in near silence.

"I found this in his shorts today." She casually placed a disposable lighter on the table.

Travis took the lighter and flicked it. A small flame emerged. He let off the button and the flame extinguished.

"Do you think he's smoking?" he asked.

"Nothing he has smells like he is. So...no, I don't think so."

He shrugged and stuck the lighter in his pocket, meaning to ask his son about it later.

She sighed and picked at her dinner. "What do you think is wrong with him?"

He shrugged again.

"School, I'm pretty sure," she added, answering her own question. "All he's ever known was Oregon. Here it must seem like a totally foreign country to him. That's pretty shocking for a teenage boy. I'm sure he's just struggling to fit in."

"I'm sure, too," Travis agreed, picking at his own dinner. *Why the hell had he dragged his family here again?* It was a question that continued to nag at him daily.

Even though it was the only offer he'd had after the incident, he realized now that he should have just said, *"No thanks,"* and found a different profession. Something far less dangerous. Something… Just something other than what he'd been forced into doing.

He stifled a belch with a fist over his mouth and sipped from his water. Even the water here was foul and disgusting, which he could almost taste in the mashed potatoes. It could just be the cloying humidity, though. Maybe that was what made everything taste so bad. Or it could be that the whole damn place just stank to high heaven. But, there wasn't much he could do about it now. Tonight, he'd finish his dinner, sit on the sofa with his wife, watch something inane on TV, and mindlessly try to forget the lousy day he'd had trying to hire a new nighttime assistant. Running the whole damn remote office on his own was a real bitch—*a real goddamned bitch.* Without Ms. Scott helping out, he probably would have quit already.

He sighed. The meal was excellent, as always. He smiled his thanks as he cleared the plates and brought them to the kitchen. Soon, he'd lose himself in some dumb TV show and doze off well before ten o'clock, get up early, and start the whole cycle all over again.

Then the phone rang.

THREE

CLEARWATER SPRINGS

THE DRIVE TO Clearwater Springs Country Club was a series of one wrong turn after another. Even the GPS on Travis's cell phone couldn't sort it out because the signal kept dropping. And he hadn't even begun to figure out the GPS system installed in the Ford Interceptor they'd given him as a patrol vehicle. Eventually, though, in between the sudden downpours and the rain letting up without rhyme or reason, he found the correct turnoff that would take him to the address he'd jotted down in his notebook. Having the windows all steamed up didn't help much, and he could hardly fathom how it could be so late—and still be so damn hot.

When he pulled into the long curving driveway, there was a man outside standing under the eaves of a covered entryway. The guy lifted a walkie-talkie out of his raincoat and said something into it. Travis eyed the guy for a moment, then collected a clipboard and got out of the Interceptor, leaving the lights on and the wipers and AC running full blast.

Immediately, water started streaming from his broad-brimmed campaign hat in rivulets, and his shirt became soaked and weighted down by the heavy downpour.

"Are you Mr. Goulding?" he asked in a voice loud enough to carry over the pelting rain.

The guy shook his head under the hood of his coat.

"Where is Mr. Goulding, then?"

Two seconds later, an elderly, balding man in a short-sleeved shirt and baby blue vest came out of the double doors and waited under the eaves close to the entrance. Travis made his way over to him, and just before reaching the eaves, the rain suddenly stopped as if someone had shut off a spigot.

"Atticus Goulding," the man said, sticking out a stubby-fingered hand and grinning wide. He was partially hunched over as if he was not able to stand up straight any longer.

Travis trapped his clipboard under his arm, stepped forward, and shook the man's outstretched hand. The old guy's grip was stronger than Travis had anticipated.

"Mr. Goulding."

"Call me Atticus," the man said, releasing his firm grip. "You must be the new sheriff we've all been hearing about. I've been planning to invite you out to the club. Once you have settled in, of course. And I must apologize that my recent invitation was offered under such...negative circumstances."

Atticus Goulding spoke with an easy, educated accent and immediately Travis connected intelligence with the man. Ever since arriving two weeks ago, all the people he'd met had had thick accents and slurred speech, which bordered on some secret language they all shared in common. It was good to finally meet someone with whom he could easily communicate with for a change.

"Call me Travis. Travis Morrison. And I'm a deputy sheriff, not the sheriff, sir."

"Ah, sorry. My mistake...Travis. I appreciate you coming tonight. I hope you weren't interrupted or overly inconvenienced."

"No, it's fine."

"Good, good. Why don't you come in out of the rain and I'll explain what's going on here."

"Is the body located inside, then?"

Atticus glanced at the man in the rain jacket. "Not exactly."

"Have the paramedics been called? I didn't pick up anything on the radio about it on my drive out here."

Atticus coughed into his fist and then pounded on his chest. "Excuse me. Why don't you come on inside now and I'll fill you in on the details? Ya okay with that?"

Travis frowned, not just for the slight backward slide in grammar, but because something else was feeling a bit squishy about the guy.

"I have to call this in to county first," Travis said. "We'll need to bring out a paramedic or coroner to pronounce time of death."

"No, no. Hold on, son. Just come on inside. I'll explain everything in a minute. No need to bring anyone else into this, just yet."

That squishy feeling now was spreading to the pit of his stomach. *Something is definitely not right here.* But, being new to the town, he didn't know where the power structures lay just yet. Now was the time to listen—not the time to dictate.

He removed his hat and shook the water off it and pointed it at the door. Atticus grinned wide, and the guy in the raincoat hurried to open the double doors for them.

Inside, the entryway was paved in rust-colored tiles. Along each wall were large photographs of the golf course and the country club grounds from above. Also along the walls were wood and glass trophy cases and photographs of various professional golfers Travis thought he recognized. But he wasn't one-hundred percent sure since he didn't play golf. He preferred baseball, or football, or basketball—anything else. Hitting and chasing a tiny ball around with a club seemed far too frustrating to be called an actual sport.

On a three-legged easel propped near an arrangement of potted plants was a poster board advertising an upcoming golf tournament. Travis ran his eyes up and down the board and did a quick calculation. He realized that the tournament would take place in ten days' time.

No wonder the guy wants to keep this quiet.

"Welcome to my golf club, Deputy," Atticus said. "Clearwater Creek has been in my family now for three generations. We might be a bit on the remote side, but we bring in only the best players and members. Our twelfth hole was rated one of the top eight in the entire state, twenty-second in the nation, I might add."

Travis nodded. He stepped to the trophy case and looked over all the cups and awards arrayed there.

"You play golf, son?"

Travis shook his head no.

"Got any kids?"

Travis cleared his throat and glanced at the man, wondering why he'd been asked and what business it was of Goulding's to know. But he saw no harm in it.

"One," he said. "A son."

"I'm sorry. I'm prying, aren't I?"

"Forget it."

"The reason I asked is—" He pointed at the poster board advertisement, "—we are having a father and son Pro-Am tournament coming up in less than two weeks. There are going to be plenty of Hollywood celebrities attending with their children. And...if your son is old enough, then maybe you both might wish to sign up. That is all. I'd be more than happy to have the club cover your entrance fees. It would be a good way for you to meet the community and them to meet you—and maybe even rub elbows with some gen-u-ine movie stars."

"Thank you. I'll consider it. Now about the man you reported?"

"Yes, yes, yes. Tragic that. Poor Harold was out on hole sixteen and dropped dead from a heart attack." Atticus raised a hand and watched it as he dropped the palm downward in one motion while shaking his head side to side. "Sadly, this happens far too often when we get these awful heat waves. This one has been nasty, to say the least."

"There was no ambulance called then?"

Atticus made a sucking sound and shook his head. "There was no need to."

Travis sighed. "I will need to see the body before I call in the coroner."

"That's already been taken care of."

"I'm sorry, what? Taken care of—?"

"Just follow me, son. I'll explain it all." He turned and began walking away, then said over his shoulder, "Can I offer you a drink? Whiskey, perhaps?"

"Technically, I'm on duty."

"I won't tell. Just one drink."

While he was tempted, Travis shook his head instead. "Thank you, sir, no."

"Suit yourself, then. This way if you please."

Travis followed the man through the clubhouse, past the pro shop, and down a corridor to an imposing office door with two crisscrossing palm trees and an alligator carved into the wood. When Atticus opened the door, the office expanded into a large space decorated in rich, dark woods that looked out over an extensive pond now lit by colored spotlights. Behind the pond, out past the reach of the lights, was a curtain of darkness. Travis thought he saw hints of the golf course far off in the gloom. *It must be a stunning view during the day.*

As he watched through the steamy windows, rain began to pelt against them and drive thick beads of water together, which then streamed down the panes of glass in random patterns.

"You sure you don't want that drink now?"

"I'm sure."

"Have a seat then."

"I'd prefer to stand."

"Okay, I understand." Atticus went to a bar with an array of cut crystal decanters. He unstoppered one and poured himself a drink.

Returning, he said, "I knew the man who died tonight. He was a regular here and one of the community's most upstanding members. He was also a nice guy, but, sadly, I always thought he drank and smoked a bit too much. Still, dying that young..." He twisted his head side to side and turned to stare out the glass. Travis watched the man's reflection in the window while Atticus lifted his tumbler in salute to something outside the glass, then drank. The ice cubes clinked together when he lowered the tumbler. "Wish I could have warned him earlier. Wish we all could have."

Travis took a breath. "And where exactly is the man's body now?"

"You know, I can tell I'm going to like you, Deputy Morrison. You're all business and get straight to the point."

"And the body, sir?"

"See...that's where the problem lies." He sucked air through his lips and raised his whiskey glass in front of him. "I'm not exactly sure where the body is now. I'm afraid it's gone missing."

FOUR

WELCOME TO THE EVERGLADES

"SO LET ME understand this. His body is now…*missing?*" Travis asked, a bit bewildered. He set his hat on the edge of Atticus's desk and opened his notepad. He checked his watch and jotted down a line concerning the event and time—*Missing? 10:22pm.* He wanted to be able to recall the precise time he was told the body had gone missing when it came time to fill out the report. *Missing body? First few days on the job? This is not going to go over so well.* He stood a little straighter.

Atticus let out a long sigh. "I'm afraid so."

"Did someone move it?"

"Not exactly. I'm assuming you are a little new to the Everglades, aren't you?"

"I recently moved here from Oregon. Yes, this is all fairly new to me."

"Oregon, you say? You're a long way from home then, son."

Travis wet his lips. "You said the body is missing?"

Atticus cleared his throat again. "See, down here we have an alligator problem. Those damn environmentalists won't allow us to hunt them here out of season. They are afraid those pests might go extinct and are more concerned about the—" He shook his head.

14

"Nevermind. That's not important. I shouldn't even bring that up when a man's death is what we're concerned with here. Regardless, those dang monsters dragged off the body before we could get to it. We haven't found it yet. Or any signs. Which is not atypical when it comes to those lousy gators."

"So your men are out there looking for it?"

Atticus held up his walkie-talkie and nodded.

"And what makes you so certain it was a heart attack that killed him?"

"Mr. Morrison—Deputy Morrison. The alligators here will generally leave people alone. They are more afraid of us than we are of them. But they are getting bolder as they continue to breed unchecked. Just too damn many of them. It is creating a real problem."

Travis tapped his pencil on his notebook. "Heart attack?"

"Yes, sorry. Just the frustrations of an old man." Atticus drew in a long breath. "Mr. Robertson had a heart attack, I was told. His companions tried to revive him with CPR. When that wasn't working, one went to fetch help while the other stayed behind. But as soon as our on-duty medic returned to where Mr. Robertson had expired, no one was there. I guess there was some confusion and the man who had stayed behind left as well, unexpectedly."

Travis stopped writing. "Confusion?"

"I was not able to get to the bottom of it."

"Where are Mr. Robertson's companions now?"

"I'm afraid I sent them all home. I apologize. I should have kept them here until you showed up, but they were a little rattled. I told them we would keep looking for Mr. Robertson, and that there was nothing they could do for him tonight."

Travis turned the page in his notepad and started another note. He was a little perturbed by the man's actions, but he also was well aware that saying anything about it now would not help in understanding what had actually happened.

"I'll need the men's names and addresses."

"Sure, sure, of course," said Atticus, waving a hand dismissively. "I'll get you all that in due time. But first—well, we need to settle up on something."

Travis stopped writing. "And what is that?"

Atticus clucked his tongue and then wet his lips. "This is a very sensitive subject, and I'm going to need your help here, Deputy. I hope I can count on you. While we can certainly report that the poor man died of a heart attack doing what he loved most, we can't report that the body...might have been eaten by alligators. I'm sure you can sympathize with our position. With the father and son event coming up, and all the planning that has gone into it, telling people about an alligator attack might cause them to worry more than they should. And I assure you, there is absolutely nothing to worry about here. Nothing at all. This was just an unfortunate and untimely event."

The way the man had said it had Travis's neck hairs tingling. "And yet we have a man who has died and no body."

Atticus rubbed the back of his own neck and gave a slow nod. "Yeah, I'm afraid so. He was an important man. We will all miss him." He bowed his head in respect.

Travis thought about it for a moment. He looked down while biting his lip. He didn't see much choice in the matter.

"We have to find the body first," he said, voice lowered.

Atticus said nothing for a beat, then, "I wish that was possible. But it may not be. We can do our best to keep the lid on this, can't we? I do need to know—and this is very important—are you with us? Are you with the community? Can we keep this business with the alligators...private? For now at least."

Travis let out a held breath. "I'll have to think about that. In the meantime, is it possible to see where—" He checked his notes because his mind was reeling with possibilities, none of them good, "—Mr. Robertson died?"

"Sure, sure." Atticus raised the walkie-talkie, punched the button on the side, and started talking.

FIVE

LEECHES

THE RAINS HELD off long enough for them to make the trip out to the sixteenth hole. The man in the rain jacket drove the golf cart while Travis and Atticus sat in silence behind him. The dim lights on the cart barely lit the way ahead, but the man driving knew the route well enough to know where he was going.

Eventually, they came to a halt, near where the grass went from short to long to almost shoulder height. The ground was soggy, and as Travis stepped off the cart, his boots sank into the soft mud, which sucked at them and threatened to pull them off.

Atticus was wearing knee-high rubber galoshes now and was carrying an LED lantern he'd grabbed from the cart.

"This is the spot where Mr. Robertson had his heart attack." Atticus held up the lantern, and there was a clear outline in the mud with many shoe prints all around it. Most of those prints were now filled with rainwater.

"I thought you said your men were out searching."

"They were," Atticus said, "right, Carlos?"

The man in the rain jacket nodded but looked a little worried. Travis kept watch on the man for a few seconds. The guy rubbed his chin and glanced away. He wasn't saying much, either. Something was definitely going on here, and Travis knew then he wasn't going to get a straight story from anyone. All he could depend on now was his own eyes and ears and nose. And the little voice in his head was warning him that danger was all around him. But the sooner he got this all over with, the sooner he could get home and crawl into bed with his wife.

He sidestepped the matted-down area while keeping his mouth closed and swatting away mosquitos that buzzed in front of his face. The depression where the man had once been seemed narrower at one end, and the ground all about it was furrowed and filled with standing water.

Instead of breaking out his flashlight, he borrowed the lantern from Atticus and began to follow the squiggly trail in the mud that led off into the marsh. He went a few steps deeper, and his boots started sinking even further, up past his ankles.

"I would advise you not to go in there, Deputy," Atticus said from behind.

Travis ignored the warning. He'd seen something he was sure would lead him to the body if he just followed it. He went another ten steps, and the world around him seemed to all but disappear and become a jungle of shadowy shapes. He was surrounded by tall plants and verdant undergrowth. The unending sounds of the insects and other creatures in the night sent chills down his spine, even as soaked in sweat as he was now. It felt a little like swimming slowly through a steam bath, and the oppressive heat and smells of decay and rot were all around him, closing in on him, smothering him.

"Deputy Morrison."

Travis ignored Atticus's call, which sounded almost far off in the distance now. He was too focused on his task. He pulled at his sinking boots and moved another step forward. Another. Something scraped against the back of his leg. He turned to see what it was.

A snake slithered past, its tail snapping against his leg. He jumped, tottered, and almost fell on his backside as he watched the slithering shape vanish into the dense vegetation, leaving fresh ripples on the water's surface.

But he had also spotted something that didn't belong there. He raised the lantern and bent forward to inspect his find. He had to push aside a cluster of leaves, and—

A man's head bobbed up in the water like a rising cork and rolled over slowly. The head was no longer attached to a body. A single eyeball remained, glazed over and bulging out and reflecting the whiteness of the lantern. The flesh on one side of the cheek had been completely stripped to the bone, and there were small brown slugs—*no, leeches*, he corrected himself—gnawing on it.

This hadn't been the first time he'd seen a dead person before, but it had been the first time he'd only found a head without a body. And the crawling leeches caused him to raise his wrist and put it against his mouth while his stomach heaved involuntarily.

Then he realized just where he was.

Oh, crap. This was a stupid idea. A real stupid idea.

He was standing in the same exact watery muck that the leeches were all in. He instantly imagined them slithering and squirming their way up inside his pants, crawling and attaching themselves with their sharp, barbed teeth, and chewing on his flesh.

Reacting more than thinking, he grabbed the bobbing head by the hair and yanked hard as he drove his legs like pistons through the water, following the same path he'd taken into the swamp, and nearly dropping the lantern as he ran. Water splashed frantically around him, and his feet kept slipping and sliding in the gooey mud, but he held on to both the severed head and the lantern as he extended his arms for balance and made his way out of the marsh and back onto solid ground.

Without thinking about it, he tossed the head aside and began patting at his legs in swelling panic, feeling around to see if any of those awful leeches had made it inside his pants and were now feasting on his flesh.

"Are you okay, Deputy?" Atticus asked, perhaps a little too calmly.

Travis didn't answer right away. He continued his hurried assessment, pulling up each pant leg while working to put his mind back in order. Finally, he ran his hands up and down his thighs but felt nothing other than soggy dampness and sticky mud.

Letting out a long, head-clearing breath, he glanced at the severed head he'd pulled from the water and noticed something strange about it. The head wasn't completely severed. The top of the spine was still attached somewhat, and one of the collarbones hung limply by a flap of skin or something else. The leeches that had attached themselves to the dead man's remains pulsed and wriggled in the reflected light of the lantern.

"Nasty buggers," Atticus said. He reached out and grabbed one of the swollen leeches, plucked it off, and tossed it into the night. It made a small splashing noise off in the distance that was barely audible over the buzzing of the insects. "Leeches? You'll get used to them. They are all over the place, but they are mostly harmless here. It's the snakes and the gators you really got to look out for. Going off into the swamp alone like that was not such a good idea, Deputy. I tried to warn you."

Shivering despite the heat, Travis again belched with a hand over his mouth to keep himself from retching.

"That's Harold Robertson, all right. Poor guy. Not much left of him now, I see, but at least we know what happened to his body. I have my doubts that we are going to find much more than this. Looks like the gators did get to him."

Does he really know what happened? Travis wondered as he stared at the man. The guy hardly blinked at seeing such a gruesome display. *What the hell is wrong with these people?*

He also wondered, with a bone-chilling effect, if there was any way in hell he could find another job—any job—that was somewhere other than *here*.

SIX

UP ALL NIGHT

TRAVIS RUBBED HIS bleary eyes and stared at the computer screen—the same screen he'd been staring at for hours. He'd not been able to figure out the new computer system yet, and instead of giving up and going home, he had just stared blankly at the login screen and its PASSWORD INCORRECT prompt in bold red letters, practically to the point of obsession.

Red was the color of blood. Red was the color staining the plastic bag with the severed head in it that was now stewing in the office refrigerator next to an old container of coffee creamer. He had nowhere else left to put the man's remains, and when he'd called the county coroner, he'd found that the coroner was not going to be able to come out and collect those remains and until at least ten a.m. There was no particular hurry on their part. *The head wasn't going anywhere,* the woman on the phone had said, and the cause of death was already known, supposedly.

But just the thought of the gruesome scene he'd encountered the previous night and the severed head now marinating in its own juices, sealed up tight in plastic evidence bags, had left him numbed to the core.

After arriving at the office, he'd changed from his damp uniform into a spare stashed in his desk, texted his wife and told her he wouldn't be home, and then put on a pot of coffee, ready to pull an all-nighter. There was no way he could sleep. Not after what he'd seen. He didn't dare close his eyes.

The coffee still sat on the burner, untouched. And there was that damn incessant blinking red error message on the computer screen. He'd tried the password that had worked the previous day over and over. It just wasn't working today, and he'd given up on it hours ago, choosing now to just watch it, as if his simple act of staring at it would change its condition.

What kind of place builds a golf course next to a goddamned swamp? What kind of idiot would play golf on a course like that? With snakes and gators and all those...godawful, slimy leeches—?

These were just some of questions he couldn't find answers to, even though he'd stared down black bears and mountain lions, and chased them off before, back in his home state. *But gators? Could I chase one of those off? Where would you even shoot them?* They terrified him to no end, and suddenly, his 9mm sidearm seemed far too small to deal with them effectively.

And another thought was puzzling him as well—the look on Atticus Goulding's face when confronted with the remains of one of his patrons. It just didn't add up like it should. Nothing was making much sense.

He blinked again and puffed air through his narrowed lips, then reached for his notebook and glanced at the names of the other two men who were with the victim at the time of the man's death—a Mr. Robert McGee and a Mr. Casper Johnson, III. According to the information Atticus had provided, the two men had been out golfing with the victim, Harold Robertson, when he'd had a heart attack. It had been Johnson who had stayed behind but had somehow wandered off before the medic had arrived. Travis had made a note on that and planned to follow up with those two men today and get statements from each—as soon as he could get into his damn computer, that was, and start all the damn paperwork.

A solid paper trail had been one item the sheriff insisted on when Travis had been given the job. It always was to come first. There was something about being under scrutiny by the Justice

Department. But the particular form he needed to fill out, he couldn't even get to because it was locked up on the stupid computer, which seemed to be mocking him now.

He tried his password once more.

INCORRECT PASSWORD, the message said.

Gah! He slapped his palms on the desktop and shoved himself back and went to the coffee maker. He grabbed a Styrofoam cup and filled it, then sniffed the brew and realized it had been sitting there a bit too long, but he had no choice other than making a fresh pot, so he dumped three sugar packets into it and stirred, then rested against the counter and glanced at the clock.

His wife would be waking up soon. As would his son. While he wanted to take his son to school today, an investigation of this magnitude was just too much for that. He'd promised his wife that he'd put his family first, but...*how can I do that now?* He wasn't sure he'd even be able to look at his son without seeing that horrible bobbing head floating in the water again and seeing his son's face on it.

He sipped the hot coffee, wanting to think of something else, or maybe nothing at all. He then set the cup back down. He just didn't have the taste for it at the moment.

A car door slammed. He sighed and pushed away from the counter and returned to his desk just before the office door opened and a very surprised-looking Ms. Beatrice Scott walked in carrying a potted plant with a red ribbon tied around it. She was his day helper and had run the office for the previous deputy assigned to this remote substation. She'd been there for years, supposedly, and had been working to hire someone else to cover the night shift, but so far had been unsuccessful in finding anyone willing to take the job.

"Mr. Morrison," she said. Her southern accent was thick and warm. "I had not expected you to come in so early." She took another step and offloaded a bulging bag on a chair back near the front of the office, next to her desk. She smiled at him and toddled over, favoring one leg, and set the plant on the corner of his desktop.

"I should have picked up one of these for you earlier. It's been just so darn crazy around here with the transition that I haven't had a good chance to welcome you yet." She twisted the plant, looked at it, then twisted it again, nodding as if it now met her approval. "So...welcome to our fine, upstanding community."

"Thank you," he replied, nodding. "Appreciate it."

Travis rubbed at the corners of his eyes and yawned.

"Have you been here all night, then?" she asked, lowering one eyebrow.

He glanced away.

"Oh, you poor boy. There's a problem, right? Why didn't you call me? I would have come in. Is there anything I can do? Anything I can do now?"

"It's...well, thank you. Maybe you can." He drew a breath. "Do you know why I can't get into this damn computer?"

She smiled a toothy grin and came around to his side of the desk. "You done tried the password I gave you?"

"Probably a hundred times."

Tsking like a correcting schoolteacher, she eyed his keyboard and, two seconds later, reached down and struck a single key—CAPS LOCK.

"Try it now."

He did and the computer accepted his password.

Closing his eyes and shaking his head in disgust, he let out a single puff through his nose. "I feel like a goddamned idiot."

She smiled at him again, this time reproachingly. She had tiny worry lines around her lips that stretched tight and relaxed as she released her smile. "Don't fret about that, deary. Happens to all of us."

He watched her for a second. "And I apologize for taking the Lord's name in vain," he said, remembering her church-going ways.

"You're forgiven," she said, her head going up and down.

"And, a good morning to you, Ms. Scott. Thank you for the...very lovely plant."

"It is, isn't it?" she said as she returned to her desk and dug into the oversized bag she had brought along with her.

He let his tension and need to play nice with her go and refocused on his computer and found the link to bring up the reporting forms, selected the first line, and then stared at the blinking cursor now on the date and time field. He paged through his paper notebook, turning it back a few pages and tried to make sense of his own writing that had been blurred by the rain. Then he stopped to wonder what date they used here for their reports. Was it the date of the event or the date the event was entered? He was embarrassed to ask another stupid question, but—

He glanced up at Ms. Scott and saw her standing in front of the refrigerator door, just about to open it.

"Wait, wait. Hold it a sec," he said as he rose, perhaps a little too loudly.

She paused and flashed him a puzzled look.

He hustled over to where she stood and put a hand on the refrigerator door.

"You have something in there you don't want me to know about?" she asked.

"No, it's not that…it's—well, yeah, I do."

She put a brown paper back down on the counter behind her and crossed her arms over her chest.

"What happened?"

"A man had a heart attack last night."

"And what does that have to do with the refrigerator?"

"That might require some explanation."

"Nonsense," she said, unfolded her arms, and tried to push him out of the way. She was a rather large woman, so, simply her presence was enough to make him shift his weight onto his heels.

"No, you probably shouldn't."

She eyed him carefully. "I've lived here all my life. There ain't nothing I haven't seen. Move aside, honey."

"You really better not."

"No, darlin', step aside. I best see what's in there."

He thought about it for a second, then complied.

She opened the door and bent forward. He felt the cool air escaping and brush against his cheeks as he bent beside her. She pivoted her head his way, meeting his eyes from only inches away.

"Gator?" she asked.

He pulled back and retreated a step, straightening. "Yes. How did you know?"

"But you jus' said it was a heart attack, right?"

"Yes."

"Hmmph. That's poor old Mr. Robertson, I'm sure. Did he go having that heart attack before or after the gator got to him?"

SEVEN

NOT FROM AROUND HERE

TRAVIS PULLED UP the long drive to the residential address he had been given for Mr. Casper Johnson. This time, his GPS took him directly to the right location. Maybe having it not working the previous night had something to do with the rains, he figured. Anyway, it had worked perfectly this time.

The house was quite large and looked more like an estate. Out front, a long silver Mercedes was parked next to a black Range Rover. Both had been washed recently and now shined brightly in the glaring sunlight.

Stepping out of the air-conditioned interior of his patrol SUV, Travis almost instantly began to sweat. The heavy air reminded him of a sauna, and the oppressive heat and humidity made it difficult to breathe. Almost as soon as he stepped out of his vehicle, a man approached, crunching pea gravel underfoot.

"You Deputy Morrison?" the man asked.

Travis nodded and bent back inside the SUV to get his notepad. When he came back out, the man was standing right next to him. The guy was impeccably dressed in a white shirt with white slacks, which contrasted with his dark bronze skin.

"Need any help there, sir?"

"I'm okay," Travis said. He turned and stuck out his hand. The man took it and gave him a puzzled look like Travis had somehow broken some kind of protocol. Then the handshake became even more vigorous and was accompanied by a smile.

"I'm to take you to Mr. Johnson, sir. He's with clients at the moment, but he'll be available shortly to answer any questions. May I offer you some iced tea or maybe a soda?"

Travis was still feeling the disorienting effects of operating on little to no sleep. "Do you have, perhaps, a Diet Coke?"

"Certainly do, sir. Follow me."

The man led him into the foyer and across what appeared to be very expensive Spanish tile. There were windows everywhere in the house, and the decorations were mostly colored in shades of light blues and pinks. They passed by various paintings that Travis was sure had cost a small fortune. Finally, they arrived at a room in the back with windows looking out over a large expanse of deep green lawn. High-backed chairs and an oversized leather sofa filled the space, which even included a fireplace that seemed woefully out of place. The room had the faint smell of cigar smoke, and there were pictures on the walls of various sports and political figures posing with whom Travis suspected was Mr. Johnson.

The man dressed in white said, "He'll be with you shortly, sir. I'll be back with that Diet Coke in just a moment."

"Thank you—wait, I'm sorry, I didn't catch your name."

"I'm nobody to be concerned about, Mr. Morrison. I just work for Mr. Johnson."

Travis paused a beat then stepped forward, putting his notebook under one arm and thrusting his hand out again. "Call me Travis. I work for the Okatee Sheriff's office now—and it's nice to meet you." He tilted his head slightly. "I think I know you..."

The man again accepted the second handshake, a bit confused. "Alshon Floyd, sir."

"Did you once play football?"

"I did, sir. How did you know?"

"You played for Notre Dame, right?"

"Yes, sir, I did," he said with a tinge of regret.

"You were quite a receiver, if I recall. I remember that game against Duke. Four TDs, you had, right? Impressive."

Alshon smiled wide. "Thank you, sir," he said. "Nobody remembers me like that."

Travis knew better not to ask any more about the man's career. It was obvious from the situation now that Alshon had either suffered an injury or had not made the NFL for one reason or another, and it was probably best not to bring that subject up. Instead, Travis just stood there until Alshon nodded.

"I'll get that Diet Coke for you right away, sir. Ice?"

"Please. Wouldn't drink it any other way."

Alshon smiled again, turned, and left.

Except for the large grandfather clock next to the bookshelves, it was deathly quiet, as if he were locked inside a bank vault. He circled the room, checking various trophies and photographs on the walls. There were some impressive figures posing with Casper Johnson. He even had a picture with the former President of the United States. But the far more important image that Travis focused in on was a picture of Don Shula, the coach of the Miami Dolphins.

"Met him years ago," a voice said from behind.

Travis whirled. The man who had spoken was obviously Casper Johnson. Travis had run the guy's license and seen his picture. The guy looked a little older, a little balder. The man standing next to him was another he recognized, Robert McGee. He planned to go visit with Mr. McGee later that day. But now he could talk with them both, which was rather fortunate—or suspicious, he also thought. But the oddest of the three was Atticus Goulding.

What is he doing here? Instantly, Travis was certain that something wasn't right about the entire situation.

"Good to see you again, Deputy Morrison," Atticus Goulding said. "I only wish it was under better circumstances."

Alshon returned, weaving his way past the men, balancing a silver tray as he went. On it was a glass with ice and the diet cola.

"Thank you," Travis said, accepting the beverage.

"Whiskeys for us—all around," Johnson said. "And, hurry it up this time, won't you?"

"Yes, sir, Mr. Johnson. Right away."

Alshon hustled from the room, spinning completely around as he weaved past the men again, the tray tipping left and right, but never in any danger of falling. When he was gone, Johnson said, "That boy sure was great—once. Had all the moves."

The other men nodded their agreements as they filtered into the room and took seats in the various chairs. Travis remained standing.

"What can we do for you, Deputy?" Casper Johnson asked.

"I'm here to collect a little more information for my official report." He opened his notebook and raised a pencil to start writing. "It was an alligator attack, then?"

The three men all looked at one another.

"No, son, it was a heart attack that killed him," Atticus said slowly. "The gators got to him after that. You were extremely lucky to find what little that you did."

Travis had considered calling the sheriff and getting a recovery team out there to see if they could locate the rest of the body, but when he consulted with Ms. Scott, she'd let him know that the sheriff would consider it a waste of resources to do so, and it would lead to far more paperwork than she thought was necessary, so he'd let the matter drop. What was important now was closing the case and getting the cause of death over to the county coroner's office, so they could start their paperwork before the coroner arrived, which now was going to be sometime around noon. Travis checked his watch. He still had two hours before he would need to return to meet the man.

He would rather have interviewed each man here separately, though having them all together like this now might save some time. But having them together like this still meant something else entirely. It was fairly obvious to all, but he suspected what remained unsaid was meant to remain unsaid. The little voice in his head was telling him to document everything in detail and play dumb. Now was not yet the time for direct confrontations.

"Heart attack," Travis said, jotting down a note on his pad. "Can either of you tell me exactly what you saw that night?"

Johnson cleared his throat. "We were out for our weekly game. Harry was going on and on about something…" He snapped his fingers and looked at Robert McGee. "Taxes, if I recall. We were agreeing with him...and then he goes and gets this strange look on his face...like he was shocked by something. And then he just collapsed." He glanced at Atticus, who nodded in sympathetic agreement.

Travis watched them all closely while writing down another note.

"Tommy, here, tried to give Harry the...mouth to mouth—umm—CPR. While he did that, I ran to the cart and started driving back to the clubhouse as fast as I could, to get help."

Travis made a note and then asked, "Didn't any of you have a cell phone?"

No one said anything for several seconds.

"Cell phones don't generally work around here when it's been raining like that. Weather. Clouds. Interference, is what they say." It had been Atticus who had said it.

Johnson looked at him and shrugged. "Yes, I'd checked mine, certainly, but—ah, here we go now."

Alshon had returned with three tumbler glasses fill with ice cubes and honey-colored whiskey. He got ready to pass them out while Travis extended his notes. These three were hiding something. That was certainly clear. But as to what that was, he hadn't a clue. He figured it was best to keep playing dumb, and maybe they'd let something slip.

"So that's like...ah...GPS signals, right?" Travis asked. "I couldn't get mine to work last night."

"Yes," Atticus said, nodding. "It's a problem we all have down here. You'll get used to it."

The three men removed their drinks from the silver tray.

"You don't mind if we drink, Deputy, do you?" Johnson asked. "We're still a little in shock over poor old Harry."

Travis shook his head. "No, I understand."

"That'll be all, Al," Mr. Johnson said.

"Yes, sir."

After Alshon had left the room, Johnson looked at Travis and added, "He's a good boy. Poor guy. Do you know who he once was?"

"No, I can't say that I do," Travis said, hoping he hadn't been overheard earlier.

"He was a true football phenomenon on his way up to the big leagues. Played for Norte Dame. All-star wide receiver. Then he tore up his hip and—" He stopped and sucked air through his teeth.

Atticus said, "I don't think Deputy Morrison here cares much about that right now, do you, Deputy?"

Travis cleared his throat. "I'd like to know a little more about what happened last night. Are you sure it was a heart attack, then? Not something else?"

Johnson leaned forward and drank from his glass. "Yes, I'm absolutely sure. Heart attack."

"Are you a doctor?"

"What are you implying here, Deputy?" Atticus asked. When everyone turned to stare at him, he nodded and said, "Go on."

Travis held up his hand with the pencil in it and shook it in the air. "No, I'm not implying anything. I just need this for my report."

"Fine, fine," Johnson said. "I am not a doctor, but I'm one-hundred percent positive it was a heart attack. I tried CPR like they said to do on the radio, thinking of that song from the old disco movie..."

"Staying Alive," McGee added.

Johnson snapped his fingers and pointed. "That's the one."

Travis made a note. It was all fairly obvious to him now that these men were lying through their teeth about what had really happened. Just the fact that they could, thinking they would get away with it, pissed him off a little. But with no evidence except a man's severed head to go on, it would be nearly impossible to know what had actually happened.

"One more question," Travis said.

"What is it, Deputy? Anything," Atticus injected, taking over the conversation again. His eyebrows went up even though his face was showing that he thought the interview should already have ended.

Travis tapped his pencil on the notepad. "What about the alligators? Isn't it a bit dangerous to build a golf course so close to a swamp filled with something so dangerous?"

The three men all looked at each other, and then began to chuckle and shake their heads.

"You're not from around here now, are you, sonny?" Atticus said. He raised his glass in a toast and all three men drank.

EIGHT

ON ICE

THE DRIVE BACK to the office was uneventful. Travis had begun to doze off in the air-conditioned cocoon of his Interceptor as the miles rolled by. There wasn't much he could do now other than file his report and wait for the coroner to arrive. Then, perhaps he could head home and catch a long nap. It would be good to get back home and see his wife for a bit, maybe he could even swing by and pick up his son from school on the way. That would give him a chance to look over the school before the dismissal bell rang.

When he arrived at the station house, Ms. Scott was there to greet him.

"Have you learned anything yet?" she asked.

"Not much. They all say it was a heart attack."

"All?"

"Yeah, that struck me as a bit odd. Both men who were with Mr. Robertson were at the Johnson residence. Along, of course, with Mr. Goulding."

"That is a bit odd. Makes one wonder, doesn't it? Lord have mercy."

"It does. How well do you know those men?"

"I've known them all since they was jus' kids. All of them are rotten, if you ask me. Never seen them at Sunday service. Too busy counting their money. But don't let me color them too much in your eyes. They are still God's children, misguided as they might be."

Travis sat down at his desk. "You think they might be capable of doing something really bad?"

She poured a cup of coffee and set it in front of him. "Who knows what they are capable of? I ain't heard them getting in trouble with the law, but I can't remember them ever having problems with Carson, either."

"Who's Carson?"

"Oh, deary. He was the man who worked here before you. I told you that, yessiday. Jesus help me, he was a piece of work. I almost quit my job here ten times over while he worked here. I can tell with you, though, things gonna be different. The good Lord lets me see."

Travis sipped his coffee and realized he shouldn't be drinking it if he wanted to take a nap later. "You think they might have had some ulterior motives? Maybe had a problem with Mr. Robertson?"

She thought about it for a few seconds. "I really can't say. I wouldn't put much past that bunch, but I jus' can't see them killing a man, either."

Travis nodded ruefully. "Well, if you will excuse me, I have a report to write." He turned to his computer and retyped his password and brought up the partially completed report.

By the time he was halfway through finding the right words for the report, the door had opened and the county coroner had shown up. He was a skinny man with thinning hair combed over and plastered to his scalp with heavy wax. He looked more like an undertaker's assistant than an officer of the court.

"Are you Deputy Travis Morrison?" the man asked.

Travis rose and shook the man's hand. The guy handed him a card, which he read to verify the man's credentials.

From behind her desk, Ms. Scott coughed into her fist. Both men turned. "Would you like some coffee?" she asked the coroner from behind her computer monitor. In the reflection in the plate glass window behind her, Travis could see she was playing cards with the computer. Solitaire. He'd played way too many hours of that game the last time he had held a desk job. He knew it well.

"No, thanks, ma'am," the coroner said. "I was told you have some remains for me to collect?"

"Yes," Travis breathed, studying the man. He went to the refrigerator and opened the door. Glanced back once at the coroner and reached inside and drew out the bag with the head in it, holding it by the squishy bottom.

"This is all we have of Mr. Robertson," he said.

The coroner said nothing, but his eyes did widen a bit.

Travis brought the head over, still supporting the bag from underneath. The liquid had all drained to the bottom of the bag and caused the plastic to envelop his hand in squishy, bodily fluids.

Swallowing his disgust, he asked, "Is there any way your office can tell if the man died of a heart attack?"

"Heart attack?" the coroner asked. "Where's the rest of him?" Then he nodded his new understanding and asked, "Gator?"

"Apparently," Travis said.

The coroner narrowed his lips, accepting the bagged head. "Well, from what I know, gators usually kill by drowning their victims, so I'll pass this over to the medical examiner and ask if he can figure it out. No promises."

"Can you put a rush on it?" Travis asked.

"Sure..." the coroner said, looking a little green himself.

NINE

TOOTH

TRAVIS WOKE FROM a nap. He'd made it home earlier than expected and planned to wake up in time to go pick up his son from school. Rubbing his bleary eyes, he shifted on the sofa and planted his feet on the floor. On the coffee table in front of him, set between a pair of unpacked moving boxes, was his cell phone. Attached to it was a yellow sticky note. He peeled it off and read the neat handwriting.

Gone to get Jeremy and ice cream. Back soon. Love you.

She knew. She always knew just what he needed. He shook his head side to side, thinking how much he loved her and that he would not be able to function without her. She had intuited how exhausted he felt and had given him an extra hour or two of sleep. He checked his phone. No messages. The coroner hadn't called yet, and it was already approaching five p.m. He thought about it for a moment, considering that it might take them another day, maybe two, before they had any results to share. All they had was the man's head to work with, after all.

Rubbing his face, he stumbled to the bathroom. He needed to shave, and he certainly needed a shower. Both would have to wait, though, because he heard the loud clatter coming from the garage as the door began to roll up. His wife and son must be home. Quickly, he splashed water on his face, rubbed it off on a towel, and then ran his fingers through his thick hair. He studied the reflection in the mirror and consider if it was really him staring back. He'd come so far and done so much in the past few months. He hardly knew up from down any longer. But, while he still felt disgusting from the long night and the fresh heat of the day, staying inside with the AC on had dried him out enough that he felt many times better than he had when he had arrived.

A car door slammed, and the door from the garage to the kitchen opened. Jeremy stepped through toting his backpack over one shoulder. Travis began walking toward his son, wanting to apologize for not being there to drop him off in the morning, nor picking him up after school. As soon as he got close, his cell phone rang. With a glance of apology at his son, he retreated back to the living room and picked up his phone from the coffee table.

"Deputy Morrison?"

"Yeah."

"This is Mike Larson from the coroner's office. We met earlier. I have an update for your report."

"Go on."

"The ME had a look at the remains of one, Harold Robertson. He made a positive identification based on dental records. DNA tests have been sent to the lab to confirm, but we will need to acquire samples from his nearest blood relation."

Travis nodded even though no one was there to see it. His wife had stayed behind in the kitchen while his son had walked past without saying a word, heading toward the back bedrooms. For a brief second, Travis felt a bit ashamed of himself for not putting his son first.

He exhaled and refocused, somewhat amazed that the identification on Mr. Robertson had been made so rapidly. With his former department, it could take days, sometimes weeks, for lab work to come back.

"Deputy Morrison...?"

"Yeah, I'm still here."

"*There's something else—it's preliminary, but the ME doesn't seem to think the cause of death was a heart attack.*"

Travis's mind reeled at the blossoming implications of what the coroner had just said. *Proof. Tangible proof.* He'd known it in his gut, but there was a big difference between a gut feeling and knowing it as a provable fact. While he'd considered the possibilities, he also considered what those possibilities would lead to—*nothing pleasant.*

"How then?" he asked.

"*The trauma to the man's trachea indicated a sudden involuntary collapse accompanied by palpating lacerations and bruising.*"

"What does that mean?"

"*It means the man was alive when he was pulled underwater. It is still possible a heart attack was the initial cause of death, but the ME is insistent that the consistency of the injuries are better correlated with drowning. And if he drown...*"

Reluctantly, Travis asked, "How about signs of foul play?"

The coroner paused for a beat, then, "*There were no obvious signs of blunt force trauma or excessive early bleeding, which would indicate he was struck in the head. But without his entire body to examine, it is impossible to tell. The ME seemed quite insistent that the man drowned. Which would mean—*"

"Alligator?" Travis interjected.

"*Yeah, appears so. There is more to it, too. I'm texting you an image. One sec...*"

The phone went silent for a moment, then dinged and showed an image on the screen. Travis zoomed the image and tried to make sense of it. It looked like a splinter of stained bone, bulbous near one end. Next to it was a metal ruler. Travis wondered if the scale was in metric or English units—centimeters or inches.

The tooth was almost half as long as the entire ruler.

He raised the phone again to his ear. "What am I seeing?"

"*That's a tooth.*"

"A tooth?"

"*An alligator tooth, to be more specific. It was found embedded in the cranial cavity of the victim.*"

"So, you are telling me that the man was attacked by an alligator, pulled into the water, and drown?"

"*Probably. There's more...*"

"More?" Travis glanced up and saw his wife coming from the kitchen. She held a beer in one hand and had just opened it. She handed it to him, and he smiled back his thanks.

"*Yes. Deputy Morrison...the tooth is the biggest example anyone in our office has ever seen before. It's almost six inches long. That's unheard of...*"

Travis pulled the phone away from his ear and looked at the image again. It looked small on the phone's tiny screen, but his mind made the necessary adjustments, and he could almost picture it now. *Six inches...? Holy moly...* He could feel the muscles of his face tightening.

"*And,*" the coroner continued, "*that would mean the alligator it came from is like nothing we've ever seen before. It must be a real monster. Huge...*"

Travis gulped from his beer, lowered the bottle, and saw his own near-panic reflected in his wife's hazel and gold-flecked eyes.

TEN

DON QUIXOTE

JUAN GOMEZ PULLED off his straw hat, wiped his sweat-laden brow, and stared up at the cloudless blue sky. The searing sun had risen nearly to its zenith and was now blanketing everything below it in suffocating heat. He was already sweating profusely through his long-sleeved shirt, and heavy beads of moisture were trickling down his back and pooling inside his work-softened, yard-sale jeans. He stank of outdoors and gasoline exhaust, wishing that he didn't.

His wife had always struggled to keep his uniform shirt clean and tidy despite their lack of any real funds to purchase a washing machine, or any other such frivolities. After he got home today, it would be no different. She'd struggle once again to drive the salty crust away and keep him smelling halfway decent for when he got up early the next day to go to work. Day after day, it was always the same ritual. The same insufferable life.

After putting his hat back on, he stole a quick drink of water from the Igloo water dispenser the golf course maintenance job provided for him, then clicked the lever to engage the blades again on the big Toro riding mower. He revved the engine and disengaged the clutch. The mower lurched forward with the blades whirling. The whole thing shook and vibrated as if it were coming apart at the seams. But it was working just as it should, and the thick grasses lining the golf course fairway were summarily scythed to a perfect height, and the remaining debris was being ejected out to one side, blowing ever closer to the marshland to his right. Occasionally, the mower would hit a rough patch and the motor on the aging machine would bog down and choke for a bit before spinning back up to full speed.

While he rode, to pass the time, he acted out scenes from the one book in his youth that had impacted him deeply and had remained with him to this day—Miguel de Cervantes's *Don Quixote*.

He saw himself as a character in Cervantes's book. In his mind, he was not Sancho Panza, the poor farmer. No, he was the dashing Don Quixote of La Mancha, a bringer of justice and chivalry and a code of conduct that had been lost in the new world. And that made his mower the mighty steed from which he could right the planet's wrongs, at least in his imagination.

He frequently pictured such daring scenes from the great story in his head and acted them out, often talking to himself using the voice of the Man from La Mancha, all while mowing the grass of that tired old *gringo* who owned the golf course. That tired old *gringo* who treated him far worse than Don Quixote ever treated his loyal sidekick, Sancho.

But Juan was used to such bad treatment. Back in his home country, he was but a lowly peasant. His family had been too poor for him to go to school past the age of twelve. He'd worked hard his entire life, and it hadn't been until he'd come to America that he truly knew what it was like to have any money to show for all his hard work. While the *gringo* paid him less than the law had said was right, what he made in a day here was far more than he had ever made back home in a month. He didn't dare complain. And soon, he and his wife would have enough to hire coyotes to bring his poor ailing mother across the two borders and to America.

Everyone was now coming to America, which made Juan Gomez often stop to wonder what would happen to his newly adopted country in the years to come. Would it become just like the country he fled? *Most likely*, was the answer he kept landing on. But that was a long way off still, and there was nothing he could do about it now.

Today, he was Don Quixote, bringer of all that was good and right to the world. When the power-hungry socialists tried to bring their evil and destructive ways here, he would root out that infestation and banish them forever to the fiery pits of Hell!

While his mighty steed continued to chomp onward, grass spewed out on the generated wind, creating mulch that he would mow again to return the nutrients to the soil. Beside him, he carried a long wooden stick with a loop of rope on one end. Oftentimes, a wayward alligator would creep onto the golf course, and part of his job was to lasso them and drag them back to their swamp. He was not permitted to kill them, as they were a protected animal. But he was allowed to kill any snakes he found, which was good—because he hated snakes. They often gave him nightmares—crawling and slithering over his naked flesh while he slept. Panting with fear, he'd awake to his wife's prodding and slap at himself all over to get the snakes to go away.

Today, though, he had seen no alligators, which was good. And no snakes, which was even better. If it kept up, and his job was completed soon, he could end his shift early and go home to his loving wife before the sun went down. A too infrequent occurrence.

Rubbing sweat from the corners of his eyes, he looked down, then up. Two men were racing toward him in an electric maintenance cart with a pickup bed on the back stacked high with chemicals. One man was the shift supervisor, a man who drove Juan mercilessly and berated him if he made even the slightest mistake. Juan straightened on the mower, and when it became evident they were coming to speak with him, he lowered the throttle and disengaged the whirling blades. The engine slowed to an idle.

The supervisor asked a question, but the man had spoken too quickly. It took a few seconds for the English words to make sense in Juan's mind.

"Spotted any gators today?" the man repeated.

Then Juan understood and shook his head. "No, *señor*," he replied.

The man lifted a radio to his lips and spoke into it. Juan couldn't hear what was being said over the idling engine, but the man lowered the radio and said, "Out by fourteen, I need you to cut space for vendor booths. Got that, Pablo?"

Juan stared at the man for a few moments, then bobbed his head up and down obediently.

"Good," the supervisor said and sped away.

As the man drove off, Juan watched him go, wishing his mower really was a giant steed, and the pole with the rope was a twelve-foot lance. Because then he'd charge that man who hadn't even bothered to learn his real name.

It took him almost an hour to cut his way out to the fourteenth fairway, but when he did, he pulled to a stop, shut off the machine, and straightened to relieve the ache in his back. He scanned the surrounding area, trying to understand just where he was supposed to mow. There were no indications, and the supervisor had not been specific as to where the vendors might set up. He thought about it for a moment, wondering if he should go ask. But he didn't want to be wrong again. That might cost him his job. And it was such a long walk back to the clubhouse, and even if he went there, he was not sure he would find that *gringo* supervisor anywhere near it.

Sighing, he stepped away from the mower. Perhaps he could figure it out on his own. He went around to the back and wet his bandana in a stream from the water dispenser and wiped the cool water on the back of his neck and mopped away the salty sweat. The machine next to him ticked in the hot sun, and the smell of cut grass and residual exhaust fumes filled most of his senses.

But he detected something else there as well.

Something…*rotten?*

It didn't smell like any kind of decaying vegetation he could remember. It was more like spoiled meat. He'd smelled that often enough back in his home country where dead bodies were left to rot in the streets. And suddenly, he became far more suspicious of danger, and his heart began to beat faster. He could feel it in his throat.

Wiping away the dripping sweat from his lips, he returned to the mower and removed his long pole with the lasso on one end. Maybe a gator had killed something nearby, he considered. Or it could be that some animal had died just off in the marsh. Either way, he wasn't about to touch it if he found it.

He wandered over nearer to the edge of the swampy area bordering the fairway, constantly on alert for snakes. There was no way he would wander into the dense vegetation where those snakes could be lurking—not with so many of them being poisonous. And, as soon as he thought of the snakes, he could almost feel them crawling and creeping all around him. His breathing shallowed and became more rapid.

He took another tentative step, stopped, and sniffed the air.

The stench was growing stronger.

Another step.

Stopped.

Stronger still.

He fought the sudden urge to return to the mower and drive it back to the clubhouse. If he did, he was sure he would be accused of not doing his job right. He had to stay and finish. There was no other choice.

Drawing a deep breath, he straightened. Don Quixote would not fear snakes, nor dragons, nor even windmills. He would be brave and not let his fear overcome him.

A shape became visible through a narrow gap in the vegetation—two amber-colored eyeballs attached to what very well could be a floating log. But Juan knew this was not a floating log. It was an alligator—a big one.

He backpedaled a step and froze.

Slowly, he began to take another step away from it.

Then—

The alligator in the water lunged, splashing water as it came at him. Juan dug his heels into the soft earth as he tried to spin around and run, but his worn-out boots kept slipping in the mud. Only desperation brought about by near panic allowed him to cover a too-short ten feet before he turned again toward the threat.

The alligator was now completely out of the water. It had stopped moving and was waiting there, mouth opening and closing while its head turned side to side. Juan figured it must be about twice as long as he was tall, which made it not the biggest alligator he had ever seen, but bigger than most. He drew himself to his full height and held the wooden pole in front of him, ready to prod the creature if it came any closer to him.

But it didn't.

Courage slowly crept back into his mind. He'd done this before, many times. That didn't make it any easier, but at least he knew what to expect.

He adjusted the lasso at the end of the pole and started moving it closer to the alligator's scaly head. The creature lay still, not moving at all now. But Juan knew that stillness did not imply it wouldn't lunge at him the second he let his guard down, so he inched forward at a snail's pace, lowering the looped end toward the creature's head.

Just a little more.

More.

He slipped the lasso over its closed jaws and yanked hard on the rope in his hand. The loop tightened around the alligator's jaws and pinched them closed. The large animal began to thrash back and forth, but Juan held onto the stick and rope tightly until the beast settled.

He was instantly proud of what he'd just done. He'd tilted at a dragon and had won the encounter. But he was now left with the sticky problem of what to do with the captured alligator. As he'd been told, he was not allowed to kill them. He could only move them and set them free. This one was big, though, and he worried that it might prove a danger to someone on the course if it were ever encountered. He also wondered how he was going to move it without any help.

He quickly came up with a plan. One he thought was good because it was so simple. He would tie the alligator to the riding mower, leave it there, and go and get help. They would probably reward him for capturing such a big threat. It might even be enough to buy his wife a new dress, and he would not have to have her suffer the indignities of wearing someone else's previously worn clothes any longer.

Tightening his grip on the pole, he dragged the alligator along behind him with all his might, digging his heels in the earth and yanking it ever closer to the mower.

But then he stopped cold.

He had smelled that terrible stench of death again. And when he turned to see what it might be, he dropped the pole with the rope and let the alligator he had captured go.

What was now behind him required his immediate, undivided attention.

Icy fear filled him, and he froze in place, unable to decide which direction to bolt. Then, not knowing how, operating on pure instinct, he chose to start running directly away from it.

What he had just seen was a creature larger than any he had ever seen before. It was almost as big as he figured a dragon might be. But this dragon had no wings.

As he ran in a direction that would take him along the straightest path away from it he could, he glanced back over his right shoulder, nearly twisting his neck all the way around to see the mighty beast. His straw hat blocked his view but quickly fell from his head when he knocked it off with his pumping arms.

And what he saw next caused his knees to go weak and him to feel as though his bones had turned to water.

He tripped and fell to the ground face first. Pushing himself up with his hands, he started forward again. But, instead of moving, he felt a terrible weight land on his legs. He tried to turn over and see what was pinning him down, but a new pain more intense than anything he had ever felt before filled his mind with sharp, brilliant flashes of white-hot agony.

The pressure on him let up suddenly, and he tried to force his rubbery legs to move again, but they seemed now to be paralyzed. He pushed hard and rolled himself over and onto his back.

And then he saw the creature in its entirety.

The imposing beast was so enormous that it blocked out the sun from the sky, leaving him in its shadow. He mumbled a prayer from his childhood, asking the Lord above to save him and protect him.

But it wasn't to be. The dragon he had attempted to tilt at had won this time.

The creature scrambled forward, scooping Juan up in its jaws. It chomped down, and huge teeth sunk deep into the meat of Juan's torso. He reached up and beat on the mouth of the monster with his fists as it reversed itself and moved backward, toward the swamp.

Juan could taste salt in his mouth and was already coughing involuntarily, spraying hot blood into the air above him and having it return and land on his face. The giant creature continued to drag him backward while he futilely beat his fists to a pulp on the thing's armored jaws.

Still, it would not release him, and his pounding became weaker and weaker, growing more feeble by the second. Soon, he felt an entirely new wetness on his backside and neck, and the ground texture changed from grass to marsh and mud.

The last thing he saw was a dirty brown blur filled with tiny bits of floating debris as the water closed in over his head, and he sank into the murky depths.

ELEVEN

THAT BIG?

AS TRAVIS HELD the phone's handset in a lazy, half-hearted grip, he listened to the scratchy music playing in the background, wondering if he should have just hung up already. He was on hold and waiting to be connected to the Marine Biology department at Florida Tech. They had said it would only take a little bit to track someone down who could answer his questions, but it had already been more than twenty minutes—and nothing. Just the lousy hold music playing on an infinite loop.

In the meantime, Ms. Scott had taken the incoming calls the office received and was pasting yellow stickies on his desk after each one. He'd pick the little pieces of paper up, stare at them a moment, and shake his head in disgust and confusion. She'd frown at him and walk back to her desk and resume her game of Solitaire on her computer.

Finally, when it seemed that no one was going to answer, he punched the button to switch to speakerphone and went to join Ms. Scott, carrying the yellow stickies. She glanced up from her game.

"So is this the normal sort of daily crap we deal with here?" He glanced back down at the note. "Is this guy serious? A reported theft of a garden gnome?" He peeled the note back to reveal the next one. "And this here is saying that someone wants to file a complaint because Burger King went and put two pickles instead of three on her hamburger?" He flipped deeper in the growing stack. "Oh, and here is a woman claiming that her dog was impregnated by her neighbor's, and she wants that neighbor to pay for an abortion now... Can they even do that?"

Ms. Scott just calmly smiled. "Welcome to Florida." She selected another card and clicked her mouse and then raised her hands in front of her and twiddled her fingers in celebration as all her cards cleared and she was rewarded with a flashing screen telling her that she'd won.

"And here we are dealing with a dead man and giant alligator?" he asked rhetorically as he shook his head on his way back to his desk.

"Honey," Ms. Scott said, bubbling with laughter, "you ain't seen nothing yet."

Travis chuckled once in sympathy with his own self-loathing. What else could he do? He was stuck here now and would have to learn to live with it. Not everyone could have the job of their dreams. His dream was to play professional baseball, but that had never materialized. He just hadn't been good enough.

"Oh, one more thing," Ms. Scott said. "Roy Foster called. He says he has information for you on Harold Robertson's death."

"Who's he?"

"Some rich white guy."

Travis made a mental note to follow up with the man. He raised a finger to ask her more about the guy, but before he could, the hold music on the phone at his desk stopped.

"*Hello?*" a voice on the speakerphone said. "*Hello,*" it repeated.

He scrambled back to his desk and quickly oriented himself to punch the right button.

"Hi there," he said as he hastily picked up the handset and put it to his ear. "Is this Dr. Anthony Galen?"

"*No, sorry. This is his research assistant. Who is this?*"

The voice had been that of a woman and not the voice of whom he had expected. Travis grabbed his jaw and pulled down on it. He had asked to speak with Dr. Galen, whom he had looked up on the university's website. The man was supposedly an expert on inland aquatic species, which Travis assumed included alligators.

"Well, hello ma'am, this is Deputy Travis Morrison of the Okatee County Sheriff's Department. I'm calling in regards to an alligator sighting. We need some background information and I was hoping you could provide it. When will Dr. Galen be available to take my call?"

"*He won't,*" the woman said curtly.

"Excuse me?"

"*Dr. Galen is currently out of the country on a research assignment.*" She'd said it with a tinge of anger in her voice as if he were expected to know that.

He drew a long breath. "Maybe you could help me then. How much do you know about alligators?"

"*More than you, I'm certain.*"

"Ma'am, I'm from the sheriff's department, and I'm investigating a possible alligator attack. A man died, and I need some additional information for my report."

"*And how is any of that my concern?*"

Travis waited a couple of beats while he counted down from five. "Is there anyone else I can speak with on this matter?"

The woman did not respond for several seconds. Then Travis heard her sigh, long and languid. "*No, I'm sorry, it's just been a rough couple of days here. What can I help you with?*"

"I have a report from our medical examiner that shows an alligator may have attacked and drowned a man."

"*They do that all the time,*" she said. "*This is their territory, after all. We are the ones invading their homes.*"

He ignored her general admonishment and continued. "But there is something else we found—a tooth. The ME found it embedded in the man's...well, let's just say he found a tooth."

"*That is nothing really unusual, either. Crocodilia will often lose teeth after they wear down enough. They are not like human teeth. Theirs will continue to grow back throughout their lives.*"

"It's not that—it's...the tooth is at least five inches long, maybe six. We need to know if—"

"That's impossible. The longest their teeth ever get is maybe two inches, maximum. Most are about an inch and a half long, if that. You sure the tooth is crocodilian?"

"Ma'am, I'm only reporting what I was told. I don't know for sure. Is it even possible for alligator teeth to be that long?"

"No, absolutely not."

He paused again. "Is there an email address or phone number where I can send you a picture?"

"Yes, though I'm sure it's only a hoax. But send it anyway."

She gave him a cell phone number, and he forwarded the picture the coroner had texted him.

"Did you receive it yet?" he asked when she hadn't said anything for several seconds.

"Yes."

"And?"

"Where are you?" she asked excitedly. *"Exactly. Right now. Can you send me an address where I can meet with you?"*

He relayed the address of the substation and heard the clattering of a keyboard on her end.

"I'll be there in five hours and twelve minutes, maybe sooner."

The phone disconnected, leaving him holding the handset and staring at it, wondering once more what the hell he'd gotten himself into.

TWELVE

GOT A PROBLEM

"MR. GOULDING, WE may have a problem," said Dennis Parker, the golf course's maintenance manager.

Atticus Goulding glanced up from the pile of work on his desk. He'd been signing paychecks and other various contracts in preparation for the upcoming father and son event. He'd just had one of the caterers cancel on him, and the scramble to find another to replace them was proving to be an impossible task on such short notice. He had calls out, but so far, none of them had been returned.

But he'd been a businessman all his life. He was used to such trifling issues. He had often juggled ten or more problems at a time—and he always came out on top.

"What is the trouble, Mr. Parker?"

"One of our men is missing, sir. We've found the Ground Master he'd been assigned to on the fairway near hole fourteen. But so far, we haven't been able to locate him, sir."

Atticus turned the page on the checkbook in front of him and signed his name on the signature line.

"Maybe he walked off the job?" Atticus suggested, now perturbed by the useless interruption.

"I don't think so, sir."

Sighing, Atticus set down his pen and glanced at his employee. "And why is that?"

"We found his hat, sir. And it's over ninety degrees out there. He would need—"

"Yes, yes, I know it is hot. But this is Florida. It's always hot. Why did you even bring this to me?"

"Sir, I didn't want to trouble you, but…"

"Go on."

"There were signs of a struggle. The grasses near the marsh were all torn up. And…we found one of the sticks used to move the alligators when we find them. It was broken in two, and the rope was missing. Sir, I think he may have been attacked."

"By an alligator? Preposterous." Atticus picked up his pen and moved on to the next check, examined the amount, and matched it with what was in the register on the other side of his desk, and then signed his name, reluctantly. "These expenses…they are adding up too quickly, Mr. Parker. If we do not do well with the upcoming tournament, we will be facing the need to file for bankruptcy, or at least lay off staff. Do you understand what that means?"

"Yes, sir. But the man? Should we call the sheriff in to investigate?"

"I'm sure our man is fine, Mr. Parker. He just ran off somewhere. You should be the first to know we can't trust those wetbacks for much—can we?"

"Sir?"

Atticus waved his hand, making a dismissive gesture. "Can't you see that I'm busy here?"

"So…what should I do, sir?"

Atticus set his pen down again on top of the check register. He folded his hands, placed them on the desk, and began tapping his thumbs together.

"Mr. Parker. If we both wish to keep our only means of income afloat, we will need to learn to ignore such trivial matters as an employee that has gone missing. I'm sure he just ran off. You have plenty more working for you, and we can always get more if we need to. I hear they are just pouring across the border now. So, I would even hazard a guess that we can lower our overall operating costs by acquiring a few more of those hard workers and letting our more expensive employees go. Am I being clear on this?"

"Crystal clear, sir."

"Good. Now I want you to take a team out to fourteen and clean up any issues we may have there. Then I want the area scrubbed spotless, and I want our course looking lush and green. We have paying customers coming tomorrow, and I want everything fully operational and safe for our guests. If not, I will hold you personally responsible for any failures." He unfolded his hands and threw a brushing wave at the twin doors behind Parker. "Now go and don't bother me again about this."

Parker nodded once, turned on his heel, and left the office, quietly bending at the waist and shutting the twin doors behind him.

Atticus Goulding examined another figure in his ledger and grumbled when he had to hunch over and sign yet another check.

THIRTEEN

PICKLES

"NO, MA'AM," TRAVIS said, "they are not liable for how many pickles are on your—"

He was interrupted by the voice on the phone and held the handset away from his ear and glanced over at Ms. Scott, shaking his head in disgust. Sound continued to pour from the phone, and he ignored most of what was being said.

When it had gone quiet for a moment, he lifted the handset back to his ear. "Yes, I'm still listening to you. Yes, you pay my salary. No, I *am* taking your complaint seriously. Completely."

Again, he lifted the handset from his ear and rolled his neck to stretch it. At least dealing with all the silly details today had taken his mind off the horrors of the previous day, which was somewhat of a relief.

Not wanting to listen to any more of the inane chatter, though, he cleared his throat and said in his most serious voice, "Ma'am, those who have wronged you will be held to account, I can promise you that. Thank you for taking your valuable time today to call and report this terrible crime..."

She started speaking again, accusing him of trying to brush her off and ignoring the importance of the situation.

"No, ma'am, I am *not* mocking you, nor ignoring you." He sighed. "We take all reports seriously here—"

He stopped talking, and the phone's handset almost rolled out of his loose grip when he saw what was coming through the office door. He juggled the handset and recovered it, then absently hung up on the woman.

"Honey, she's only going to call back," Ms. Scott commented.

"Then you take her call and deal with it." Travis rose from his chair, shoving it backward as he headed for the front of the office.

A short woman with mousy features, thick glasses, and shoulder-length brown hair came through the door. She had a duffle bag slung over one shoulder, weighing her down. The look of eagerness on her face could best be described as a kid who was first in line and waiting to get into Disneyland.

"Are you Deputy Travis Morrison?" she asked. "I am here to see Deputy Morrison. Is he here? Right now? Is he?" Her voice was like a machine gun filled with words.

Travis stopped next to Ms. Scott's desk, who chuckled up at him, able to read the young woman and his reaction to her like a book. *She is going to be a bundle of fun*, he thought with a wee bit too much sarcasm. *Just what I need now.*

"I…"

"Well, either you are, or you aren't who I'm looking for. Is Deputy Morrison here?"

"Yes, sorry," he said, wiping his palm on his pants leg to dry it. He put his hand out and she took it, keeping the pressure light, and only giving one shake before she was off and speaking again.

"Hello there. I'm Maggie Fisk from Florida Tech. You called me. Earlier. Remember? Now where is that crocodilian tooth you sent me a picture of? Is it here? Where is it?" She glanced around the office, lifting herself on tiptoe to look past him.

She had the deepest blue eyes he'd ever seen. They were almost the color of a sapphire and were magnified by her thick glasses. Her hair was brown and her skin pale, and she wore bright red lipstick on her thick lips, which stuck out slightly, almost…pouty. She couldn't have been more than twenty-four years old, and if he didn't know any better, he would have thought she was a librarian and not a marine biologist as she had said on the phone when she had called from the road to confirm her arrival time, wanting to make sure he was going to be there when she showed up.

He sucked air and released her hand to rub the back of his neck. "Nice to meet you, Maggie. I—um—the tooth I had shown you—it is not here right now."

"So where? Where is it?"

"It's at the county office, which is about an hour's drive from here."

"Why didn't you tell me that in the first place before I drove all the way down here?" She let out a huff of resentment, then one of resignation, all in the matter of a couple of seconds. "But I'm here now, so why don't you tell me all you can about the tooth and this supposed crocodilian attack. What can you tell me about it? Anything?"

Finding a short break in her rapid onslaught of words, he injected, "You didn't give me a chance to say anything on the phone."

She drew back. What he'd said elicited a slight tug at the corner of her mouth, and she reached up and brushed a lock of hair over her right ear while looking down then up.

"Oh, fair enough," she said. She dropped her duffle bag in a chair by the front door and ran her fingers through her hair, this time pulling both sides back over her ears and pulling it behind her.

Travis rubbed his chest with his thumb, realizing she was making him nervous.

"Coffee?" Ms. Scott offered. "Soda? Water?"

"Do you have any green tea?" Maggie asked.

He almost let out a sigh of relief when she refused the coffee. She was already a bundle of energy. With a cup of coffee in her, that energy level might go even higher. He wasn't sure he could handle that at the moment.

"We just might have some tea," Ms. Scott said with a sparkle in her eyes. "Though, nobody here usually drinks tea, darling. But let me see what I can find."

"Green tea," Maggie repeated. "If you have it."

While Ms. Scott went off to dig through the cabinets in search of tea bags, Travis gestured toward a chair in front of his desk and followed Maggie as she sat. He rounded her and climbed behind his desk and sunk deep in his chair. Even with the air conditioner unit behind him blowing full blast, he was already feeling the first beads of sweat forming on his upper lip. He glanced at the picture of his wife and son on the desktop then back at the short dynamo in front of him called Maggie Fisk.

"Can you tell me anything else about that tooth?" she asked. "Anything at all...?" She did not quite know where to put her hands and was folding them and unfolding them in her lap before again brushing her hair back over her ears. "You said it came from an alligator, right? Did anyone actually *see* it?"

"A man died here," Travis said, part for her benefit, part for his own, wanting to tamp down the pace of the conversation a bit.

"I understand that," she said. "I'm sorry. I really am. But attacks by indigenous crocodilians are nothing new in these parts of Florida. You must not be from here, originally. Are you? Where are you from...? Nevermind. Not my business." She crossed her short legs and adjusted the khaki shorts she was wearing. Her shirt was unbuttoned over her T-shirt, which itself seemed to be a skeleton of some sort of prehistoric creature.

"No," he said, "it's okay. We just moved here. With my...wife and son."

"From where?"

"Oregon."

"Why in the *hell* would you do something as stupid as that?"

He ignored her. "The alligator? We have a man who was reported to have died from a heart attack, but the medical examiner is now telling me the more likely cause of death is...drowning."

"And they found that tooth exactly where in his body?"

He sucked a breath. "I'd rather not say."

She cocked her head to one side. "Why not?"

"What was left of the man was not too much. So..."

"How much exactly?"

He drummed his fingers on his desk, trying to decide just how much he should tell her. Then, recalling his conversation with the woman about how many pickles were on her hamburger, he decided to tell her everything he knew—if only to get his mind off that issue with the pickles.

He tapped the side of his head. "It was embedded in his cranial cavity. His skull."

Her lips pursed. "And what about bite marks or any other tissue damage to his torso or thighs? Crocodilia...um...alligators prefer to shake their victims to death and let them rot a bit before they tear them apart and consume them. So there might be some additional evidence I can gather if you show me the man's remains. All of them. Or whatever parts you have remaining. Yeah, that would be okay."

"About that..." he started. "We only have the man's head."

"*Oh?*" She sat back in her chair and adjusted her legs, seeming a bit surprised. "I had no idea. So all that is left is the man's head? No other tissue? Did you find a leg or an arm, or any other appendage?"

"Yes. I mean, no. I mean... What the examiner had displayed evidence of a collapsed throat—ah—trachea, and there was scarring there, too."

"I see. That is consistent with drowning, all right. It's caused by an involuntary muscle spasm that closes the throat up tight and prevents water going into the lungs." She clutched her own throat. "Most land-based mammals have such a reaction to drowning."

Travis had heard that once before, but never really believed it. They'd had a number of drowning cases back in Oregon, but most of those had been accidental, or tangentially related to alcohol. He'd never gotten close enough to the investigations to know about the throats closing up, but it seemed logical.

No one said anything for several seconds, which felt almost like a relief. Then Ms. Scott set a cup on the desk in front of Maggie, and nodded at her.

"Thank you," Maggie replied, recrossing her legs and adjusting her glasses. "Now, what was it again about the victim you mentioned? Since this guy had the number one classic sign of drowning, who is stupid enough to be calling his death a heart attack? And why was there a crocodile tooth stuck in his head?"

"Crocodile tooth? Not alligator?"

"Yes, most definitely. Both, really. Maybe something else. Crocodilian, of some sort. That's for sure. And I haven't seen a tooth that big since we were sent a fossilized sample from a *Sarcosuchus imperator*."

"What's a Sarco-o-s—what is it?"

Her eyes lit up behind her glasses. "Something—that is supposed to be extinct..."

FOURTEEN

CERTIFIABLE

THE DRIVE BACK to the golf course with Maggie Fisk riding shotgun in the Interceptor was uneventful—except for the troubling phone call Travis received right as he turned into the mile-long driveway leading to the clubhouse. Ms. Scott had called his cell phone and reported that the woman complaining about the shortage of pickles on her hamburger had returned to the restaurant and was quote, "acting crazy."

Crazy, Travis thought. *Certifiable, more likely.*

"We need to make a quick detour," he said to his passenger.

"Why would we do that?" Maggie replied, not even trying to hide her irritation.

"There's a situation I need to take care of first before it spirals out of control."

"Sure, fine whatever. Just drop me off here. I'll walk the rest of the way."

He pulled over to the side of the two-lane driveway and stopped. Then he reconsidered. Letting her go in unannounced and uninformed would surely tip his hand with the owner of the club. He wasn't about to let any of his suspicions be known yet.

"One sec..." He lifted his cell phone and dialed. "Ms. Scott...I'm going to need you to go and handle the situation with that woman at Burger King."

"*I not supposed to do that. I'm just the—*"

"Yes, you can. In fact, I think you would do a far better job than I would. I might end up shooting the poor woman."

There was a long pause. "*That's not very funny, Mr. Morrison.*"

He realized his rather tasteless joke had fallen flat. Ms. Scott was fully aware of what he'd done back in Oregon that had caused him to move to Florida, and had said she was sympathetic, but he was not entirely sure that she was. And this entire situation with the pickles was utterly ridiculous to begin with. She could handle it on her own. He was sure.

"I'm asking for a favor here," he said into the phone. "Just take care of this. Please. I'm almost at the golf course now with the biologist. I'd have to drive all the way back into town. It'd be at least twenty minutes."

He heard her huff on the other side of the line.

"*Very well. I'll go see what I can do.*"

"Thank you. I owe you one."

"*Honey, you'll owe me more than one after this. I best see you and your lovely family in church this Sunday.*"

"Yes, ma'am," he said.

"*Oh, and one more thing. We had a disturbance call a little while ago. Old Ely is at it again.*"

"Ely?"

"*He's some crotchety old gator hunter. Whole town knows about him. But I guess one kid didn't. Guess old Ely got his drink on last night and threw a punch at a kid in an Army uniform. Ely was a Marine, you see and—*"

"I'll look into that, too. Just not right now, okay?"

"*You the boss,*" she said and hung up.

"What was all that about?" Maggie asked.

"Pickles," Travis replied as he put the SUV back in gear and stepped on the gas.

"Pickles?" she repeated.

"Don't ask."

They arrived in the small parking lot in front of the main entrance. He pulled through the loop and parked close to the glass front doors. All the other parking spaces were filled, including the handicapped spaces. There were even people parked on the sides of the road leading in, and no vacant spaces were left anywhere.

"What's going on here?" Maggie asked. "Wasn't there an attack just the other day? They shouldn't be here." She started shaking her head back and forth in disbelief. "No. This is bad. Very bad. You have to warn them."

"I don't know what's going on here," Travis said, exiting the vehicle. "But I damn well intend to find out. Come on. And, please, let me do all the talking. Okay?"

"Sure," she said.

"No, I mean it."

"Sure," she said again, unconvincingly, but it was the best he figured he'd get from her.

They made their way through the entrance and back to the pro shop where they inquired on the whereabouts of Mr. Goulding. The guy next to the cash register let them know that the club owner was out in the dining area overlooking the first tee box.

When they left the cool interior and exited on a second-floor deck, Travis spotted the man he wanted to speak with sitting at a table overlooking the course. Atticus Goulding was resting comfortably under a large umbrella that shaded his table. With him were three other well-dressed men. All three had iced drinks in their hands, and as soon as Atticus spotted Travis, the laughing joviality between the men came to a withering halt.

And that casual friendliness Atticus was sharing was quickly replaced with a phony one. Travis noted the change and put on a fake front of his own.

"Gentlemen," he said as he approached.

Instead of focusing on him, all four men rose from the table to greet Maggie Fisk.

"Well, hello there," a man in a mint and white Hawaiian shirt said.

"John Frakes," another said. "Pleased to meet you."

"My friends," Atticus started, drawing everyone's attention back to him. "This is our town's new deputy...Travis Moremon...?"

"Morrison." Travis also noted the faked slight.

"Ah, yes. I apologize."

Each man held out a hand to shake Travis's while continuing to focus on Maggie, smiling and nodding at her in turn.

"And this is Maggie Fisk," Travis stated. "She's a marine biologist specializing in reptilian behavior. She's helping me with the investigation into the death of Harold Robertson."

"Tragic, that," said a man in a light blue button-up shirt and white Bermuda shorts.

"Yes, tragic," another agreed, raising his glass in salute.

Travis had been watching them all carefully. Only Atticus showed any level of surprise when Maggie had been introduced, which confirmed his suspicion of the man. But, again, now was not the right time to confront him.

"I'd like to see where the crocodilian attack took place," Maggie said.

No one said anything.

"Alligator," Travis added. "She wants to know where the..." Travis coughed into his fist. "Remains were located."

"Oh, of course, my dear," Atticus responded, voice dipping in sympathy, "but it was not an alligator attack. I'm sure the deputy has informed you that our poor Harold died of heart failure and had the indignity of having his body...dragged away by that alligator. As they are wont to do, of course."

"Of course," she repeated. "Whatever you say. Regardless, I want to see where the body was found. You should also know that you should close this course right away. After an attack like that, there may be another killed if you—"

"There won't be," Atticus interrupted. He turned to the men he had been drinking with. "Excuse me, gentlemen, this will only take us a brief moment. Enjoy yourselves while I am gone...but not too much."

Finishing a chuckle with the men, Atticus came out from under the shade of the umbrella and gestured back to the glass door leading inside to the bar area.

Once inside with Travis and Maggie, Atticus stopped, glanced at his feet, and then looked up at Travis.

"Now, Deputy, I thought I had explained to you everything that has happened already. Harry died of a heart attack. That's final. I do not appreciate you coming back here with false tales of danger from someone so..." He let it trail off. "This matter should have been closed yesterday. Your predecessor would have filed the report by now and gone back to taking care of the town's business. We have a big tournament to prepare for, and I'm sure you are busy with the security plan that needs to be filed with the town council by tomorrow morning, yes? Am I clear?"

Travis rubbed his jaw and played dumb. "Sorry. I was...unfortunately not made aware of any security plan that was needed as of yet, but I'll look into it. And yes, you were clear. I was simply asked by the coroner's office to include Ms. Fisk in the report so there would be no misunderstandings. According to the background information I received on Mr. Robertson, he was a wealthy man in good health, and if the investigation for the death certificate is not thorough enough, there could be issues with his estate distribution and insurance policies."

Atticus studied him for a moment, then nodded. "Very well. Give me a couple of minutes to call my man around. He can bring you back to the place where we located Mr. Robertson's remains. I would appreciate it if you could use discretion, as we have people on the course today, and you can certainly understand the alarm it might cause if they believed they were in any kind of danger. In the meantime, feel free to have a drink at the bar." He snapped his fingers and pointed at Travis and Maggie, catching the bartender's attention. The man behind the bar raised a hand in understanding and made a firing-gun gesture.

"You should close the entire course," Maggie said. "It's too dangerous with—"

Atticus waggled a finger in her face. His entire visage went from friendly to barely contained anger in a heartbeat. "Listen here. I will not be closing..." He trailed off and shifted his weight onto his heels. Again, he was the friendly old man. "It would be a big mistake for this town to close the course right now. I'm sure Deputy Morrison agrees, don't you, Deputy?"

Travis nodded slowly, only to see Maggie turn to him with a look of confused disappointment on her face.

"Good," Atticus said.

Travis watched the old man walk away, favoring his right leg. As soon as he and Maggie were alone, she turned to him.

"That old fart is full of shit," she said. "Heart attack, my ass. This course needs to be closed. I'm sure of it. One hundred percent positive."

Travis nodded again while biting his bottom lip in consideration of just how far he could push things.

Not too far, he figured.

FIFTEEN

BIG GUN

A MAINTENANCE WORKER by the name of Dennis Parker drove them to the place Travis had been when he'd found the severed head. He still had memories of that gruesome discovery and shuddered in revulsion as they approached the edge of the swamp.

"What's wrong?" Maggie asked, hand going to his shoulder but not touching it.

He said nothing.

"Anything else I can do for you?" the maintenance worker asked as he stopped the cart and started tapping a hand on the steering wheel. "I have to see to another job, and then I can return for you in—" He checked his watch, "—an hour?"

"That should be plenty of time," Travis said. "Right?"

This time, Maggie said nothing. She was too busy circling around behind the golf cart. She struggled to unload a duffle bag that she'd brought along.

The man on the golf cart said, "Just keep an eye out, will you? Wouldn't want you to get hurt. You're now deep in the fairway and might have to duck the occasional wild ball." He smiled crookedly, waved, and drove off.

Travis could almost feel that a golf ball was about to peg him at any moment, but he had oriented himself and knew enough about golf to keep an eye on the hole's main tee box about a hundred yards away.

Maggie unzipped the duffle bag and began to withdraw various items from it. Travis wiped at a bead of sweat with his thumb and joined her. Next, she drew out a pair of wader boots, then some sort of netting, a few plastic sample bags, and then—

Travis bent and picked the item up. It was a very large revolver in a form-fitting leather holster. He pulled it out to check it, his eyes going wide. The gun was a .44 Magnum with round-nosed bullets visible in the cylinder. He could hardly imagine Maggie firing such a huge hand cannon. Even *he* would have trouble controlling the recoil. The tiny 9mm on his hip seemed almost childish by comparison.

"Don't touch that!" she said.

"Big gun," he replied.

"Big crocodilians—*er*...gators in your parlance. Those things are extremely dangerous. I would prefer to have a hunting rifle or bangstick, but it's too hard to carry one while wading through the water, using both hands for balance."

He thought about it for a second. "Do you have a permit for that gun?"

"Permit?" she asked, eyebrow going up in questioning confusion. "Why would I need a permit?"

Then Travis put it together. He was in Florida now. Different culture, entirely. But it still didn't make much sense to go wading about looking for trouble packing so much firepower.

"Plus," she added. "That tiny gun you have strapped to your hip will just make them mad." She shook her head. "You don't want to make them mad. No. That would not be good."

She kept pulling more things from her bag that he did not recognize. But he also realized that she had brought along waders, whereas he had not. That meant either she was going in alone, or he was going to get soaked again by that stinking, brackish water.

What's my wife going to think? Two uniforms stinking and stained in a week? No, she's not going to be happy about that at all.

"Just how much do you know about crocodilians?" she asked while she worked.

He knew virtually nothing about them. He'd done a few web searches while back at the office, but that had turned up so many links he hadn't known where to start. He was a little embarrassed to admit that he knew so little about them other than the basics, so instead of answering, he remained silent.

She spun around and sat and began to pull on her waders. "They can be dangerous, but if you know what you are looking for and stay out of their way, they will generally leave you alone. One thing I should note. If they come at you, don't run away from them in a straight line. Zig-zag, if you can. They are fast but can't turn well. Unless they are in the water. Don't ever get the dumb idea that you can run or swim away from them if they trap you in the water. Best thing to do is shoot them dead."

"Isn't that illegal?"

"Technically, yes. I hate guns, but which is preferable—getting eaten alive or getting fined? And are you planning on giving me a ticket?" She waited a beat, and then said, "No, I didn't think so."

"What about the game warden? Don't they have a problem with shooting alligators?"

"Just what sort of cop are you?"

She was right, he realized. His apprehension over going back into that swamp was taking away his abilities to reason.

"You're right," he said, trying to put it behind him.

"Damn straight, I'm right," she said. She stood back up and fastened the huge revolver to her hip. It looked almost comical there.

"Okay," she continued, "I'm going to have a look around. I'm assuming you are not coming with me, but if you hear a loud bang, wait for me to yell 'clear' before you come running. And…" She looked him over, head to toe. "Everything's going to be okay. I'm an expert. I know what I'm doing."

SIXTEEN

BOYS WILL BE BOYS

YES, MAGGIE FISK was an expert in her field, but, Travis wondered, was she prepared for what might just be lurking out there in that swamp? The woman had more self-assurance than many of the women he'd met, and it intimidated him a bit. She was not big physically, but she had a way about her that made him feel small by comparison. While he knew he shouldn't let it bother him, it did. But he also figured he would just have to suck it up and get over it because there was now a golf cart full of people currently heading his way.

"Howdy," a man in a mint green polo shirt said from the front of the cart. "What's going on here?"

Travis felt a bit exposed waiting there by the edge of the swamp in his sheriff deputy's uniform, sweating bullets in the hot Florida sun.

"Nothing," he said to the man. "Routine check."

Two kids riding in the back of the cart spun around and lifted themselves in their seats. "He's seen a gator, I'll bet," one of the kids said, then turned to the other boy next to him. "Bet it's big enough to eat you."

"Hey," the man driving the cart said, "none of that talk."

"But...Dad, gators eat people. We seen it on TV. Some kid got—"

"Shut up," the younger of the two boys said. He put his hands over his ears and shook his head.

"No, you shut up," the older boy said, pulling the younger one's hand away from his ear. "I'll bet you would taste good to a gator. But you wouldn't even be a snack!"

"Dad!" the younger one yelled and started crying.

"Goddammit, boy, shut the hell up and stop teasing your brother." He jerked his thumb over his shoulder, pointing at the kids. "You got any boys, officer?"

Travis nodded his head. "Just one," he said. He came around to the back of the cart, knocked his hat forward, and put his hands on his hips. He dipped his head at the youngest of the two boys, and said in his best drawl, "I'm here to make sure no gators ever come get you, son. I'll shoot 'em before they get close. No need to get upset about it." He jerked his thumb at his chest. "No gators are gonna get any of you while I'm around." He felt a little silly saying that while in uniform, but he knew from his own son that at the age these two kids were, and all the cartoons they'd probably watched, it would connect with them better if he played the role they expected.

The little boy stopped crying and wiped under his nose. Then he spun around and smacked his older brother in the side of the head. "See!" he yelled.

"Ow," the other said and smacked his little brother in the back of the head.

"Stop it!" the man in front bellowed. "Or we're going home now."

Both boys stopped grappling and slowly complied.

"Kids," the man said, head shaking. He reached into a cooler on the seat beside him and drew out a bottled water. He handed it to Travis. "Here. Thank you for your service," the man said and drove off toward the green off in the distance.

Thank you for your service? Travis repeated in his mind as he watched the cart crest a rise. *Wasn't that a military thing?* He'd never served in the military. Not that he didn't want to, but he'd gotten married right out of high school, and his wife would have killed him if he had signed up and gone overseas. Not many from his high school had gone into the military. In fact, the prevailing mindset in his hometown was anti-military—and they told anyone who would listen, incessantly.

He chewed on this thought while drinking from the water bottle. But a new thought was making its way to the forefront of his mind. It had been at least twenty minutes since Maggie had disappeared into the swamp. He hadn't heard a thing from her since.

After screwing the lid back on the water, he stuck it in his back pocket and went as deep into the swampy area as possible. He scanned as far out as he could see, but saw no movement.

He raised a hand to his cheek and was just about to yell for her when—

His cell phone rang.

He pulled it from his pocket, checked the caller ID, and answered.

"*What time will you be home for dinner?*" It was his wife.

Absently, he said, "Not sure. Six, maybe. Might have company, too. Just one who is helping me with a case. I'm not sure how much she eats, but she is pretty small, so probably not much."

"*Oh?*" Colleen said. "*Okay, how does roast chicken sound? Mashed potatoes. All that.*"

"Fine. Love you."

"*Love you, too. And don't be late.*"

He pressed END and stared at the phone. *That's odd*, he thought. *Hadn't Atticus Goulding said that the phone reception here was poor to non-existent?* But the phone in Travis's hand was showing a solid four bars of signal strength. *Could the rains really cause that much interference?* It didn't seem likely.

After making a mental note to check coverage with the phone company, he set the cell phone back in his pocket and crossed his arms over his chest. He'd seen movement, so he backed up to where the ground was not so mushy, and waited.

Maggie Fisk came wading out of the swamp, pushing aside the dense vegetation to clear a path. She was nearly out of breath, and even in the stifling heat, her features were ashen—as if she'd just seen a ghost.

"You've got to close the entire course," she said. "And you've got to close it *now!*"

SEVENTEEN

DANGEROUS

"WAIT A MINUTE," Travis said. "We can't get hasty about this. What did you see? What evidence do you have that we should shut everything down?"

"This," Maggie said, pulling up beside him. She lifted her cell phone and showed him a picture on the screen. He bent lower and cupped his hand to block the glare.

What the—?

In the image was a footprint of sorts, but it was hard to make out as there was just a depression in the muddy ground that looked somewhat like a handprint.

"What is it that I'm seeing?" he asked.

"That," she replied proudly, "is the print from the hind foot of a crocodile. See the five toes?"

"Alligator, you mean? Or—croc-o-dillia, like you said?"

"No, that's a crocodile. A very, very big one. Bigger than they have in Africa."

He examined the image again. "And...?"

"And...?" she said with astonishment. "And...? Crocodiles do not ever come this far inland. They prefer a saltwater environment.

It's almost unheard of to see one here. Look…" She pointed at the image where the fingers or toes would normally be.

Travis didn't quite know what he would call them, toes probably, since they were on the hind feet.

She traced the outline with a fingernail. "An alligator's hind feet are webbed, whereas crocodiles do not have webbed feet."

"Is that the only difference between them?"

"No, there are others, but…this is all I had to go on."

"Why is this one so unusual then? Why the…?" He couldn't find the right word for it.

She sighed and stepped away from him, shoving the phone in her front pocket. She went over and opened her duffle bag, pulled out a hardcover book, and tossed it at him. He caught it and examined the image and title on the front.

A Children's Illustrated Guide to Reptiles—Alligators and Crocodiles.

"That should be about your level, I suppose," she said derisively.

He let the slight roll off his back and opened the book and thumbed through the pages.

"Can you just summarize it all for me? Why is it we need to worry? I thought alligators…uh…crocodiles were normal and a way of life in this part of Florida?"

This time, she double-sighed and rolled her eyes. "I don't think you are actually able to understand me. Can't you see just how big that thing is? Crocodiles are often larger than alligators, yes, but this one is so far beyond anything I have ever seen before. Look at the picture again. Closely."

She whipped out her phone and showed it to him again. He studied the image. Then he saw it. *Is this what she means?* With his fingers, he expanded the image and zoomed in tight on one of the extended digits. In it, he saw the faint outlines of something else.

A bootprint? He glanced down at Maggie's feet. She lifted one of her boots and nodded. "Yes," you get it now. "My entire foot fits in the outline of just one of its hind toes."

"That would make it…" he started to say.

"A monster?" she said excitedly. "A giant, freaking, huge monster? Ya think…?" Her hands went in the air, and she spun a quarter turn then paced a step then spun again to face him. "Do you understand what I'm saying to you now?"

"I think so."

"*Good.* That thing must weigh at least four tons, maybe six. That's like ten thousand pounds of man-eating, apex predator lurking out there. The biggest crocodilian the planet has ever seen was a *Sarcosuchus Imperator.* I told you about them earlier, remember? This thing is almost that big. But those things have been extinct for millions of years. Millions." Her hands flailed as she spoke, and Travis leaned back slightly to avoid being struck. "And, yes, it is a crocodile, *not* an alligator. Most definitely. Don't you get just how dangerous this entire situation is?"

Travis normally considered himself a smart guy. Sometimes his wife would differ with him on that, but, in the end, he was certain he was at least of average intelligence, maybe slightly above average. But, at times, he was a bit slow on the uptake. This was one of those times. And, finally, all that she was saying was chipping its way through the rock and into his brain.

"Dangerous," he repeated, nodding to himself. "Close the golf course," he mumbled, thinking of all the implications and all the troubles that now lay ahead of him.

EIGHTEEN

EVENT INTERRUPTUS

"NO, I WILL not be closing any part of the golf course," Atticus said from behind his imposing office desk.

Travis had repeated what Maggie had told him about the alligator—correction, *crocodile*—she had found. She stood next to him, practically bursting with suppressed excitement, while he thought of what he could possibly say to convince the man.

Before he could speak, Maggie blurted out, "You have to close the course. *Everything.* Do you know what you have out there? It is far too dangerous and far too special and valuable to continue to operate a…golf club." She'd said the last part with disdain. "And if you don't close it, someone is seriously going to get killed."

"Now, now, little girl," Atticus said dismissively and with mocking politeness. "You have no proof of any of this."

"I have plenty of proof. We showed it to you already."

"And I'm supposed to believe some picture you have taken of mud? How am I to know you didn't fake it and are only doing this because you are upset over our policies here?"

"Policies? What policies? Allowing your golfers to become fodder for that—? For the—?" She pushed forward, and Travis barred her way with his outstretched arm so she couldn't make it around the desk.

"You see, Deputy," Atticus said, "it really is about our policy. But that policy is in place for a reason, and we have no plans to change it, lawsuit or not."

Travis had no idea what the hell he was talking about, but he didn't want Atticus to know that, so he remained mute until he could put the pieces together.

"Our event," Atticus continued, "will proceed without interruption. We are deep in preparation for it as we speak. Haven't you seen all the father and son teams out there practicing and preparing for the tournament?"

Travis nodded. "I have."

"Good," Atticus breathed. "And I've had no reported sightings of any gators anywhere on the property in days. So, having you raising the alarm is completely unfounded. And, here, to ease your mind I'll check again just to be sure."

Atticus reached for a two-way radio on his desk and raised it in front of his mouth. "Mr. Parker, come in, please."

A few seconds later came the crackling response, "*Yes, go ahead.*"

"We have Deputy Morrison in my office informing me that there may be a large alligator loose somewhere on our property. Have you or any of your men seen anything? Anything at all?"

A few seconds later, "*No, sir. Nothing at all.*"

Atticus set the radio down on the desk. "See?"

"But it is still out there. I'm sure of it. And it has killed a man already."

Atticus dropped his fist on his desktop, not hard, not soft. "I've had just about enough of this, young lady. Mr. Robertson tragically died of a heart attack. It was only after he had expired that the alligator dragged him back into the marshes and defiled his corpse in a most gruesome way. But that is what they do—do they not?"

"You are so full of shit," she said bluntly. "If you don't close down this course and get everyone off it immediately, then they will be in danger of being attacked and killed."

"Deputy," Atticus said, shifting his gaze to Travis. "Can you really do anything here? Unless either of you can prove the dangers of this supposed giant alligator, then you will need to close this matter once and for all." He started a throaty chuckle, head shaking. "This is truly inventive of you, missy, but I've been dealing with your kind all my life. Just because we won't allow young girls to golf with their fathers in our father and son tournament is no reason for you to come in here spinning wild lies trying to scare me into shutting it down."

Atticus tapped his index finger on the blotter in front of him, then stopped. "We are done here."

"Fine," she said. "See if I care. Crocodiles don't care. They don't think. They act. If they are hungry, they'll eat anything or anyone. Even little kids. And I probably shouldn't say this, but they especially like young children because they are such easy prey. Much easier than adults. And their blood will be on your hands."

He pushed himself back in his chair. "We will have plenty of private security on hand in case there are any problems with alligators, I assure you. In the long history of this course, we have never had one of our patrons attacked by an alligator before. So, no, we are not going to close. Now go. Be gone. I'm a busy man."

"And," she continued, not backing down, "sometimes they can be territorial as well. We've invaded their home turf, which they will seek to defend at all costs."

She continued to rant about territories and the destruction of natural habitats, but it soon descended into a jumble of big words that Travis did not fully understand, nor did he care to as they were not important nor related to the conversation.

When she finally stopped talking, Atticus's angry gaze remained affixed on her, and then broke off, and he resumed checking through the pile of paperwork on his desk.

Travis shuffled uncomfortably on his feet, knowing the meeting was now officially over. There was no real way they could win the argument and be allowed to shut down the golf course. He'd pretty much known this from the start. It had been a long shot but still worth a try. He only hoped his connection with the man in front of him had not been injured too much. The last thing he needed was to have the guy calling the sheriff and blocking any actions Maggie wanted to take to continue her investigation, or that might get her thrown off the property entirely, which wouldn't necessarily be a good career move for him, either.

"We should go," he said to Maggie.

"Fine," she said, then grunted under her breath. She then grabbed him by the elbow. "I need to get back to collect a couple of things from my car. Are you coming or not?"

NINETEEN

TURNABOUT

TRAVIS PRESSED THE END button on his cell phone to disconnect the call and climbed into the driver's seat of his Ford Interceptor SUV.

Ms. Scott had called a few seconds ago to inform him that he had three outstanding issues that needed to be followed up on soon—a reported burglary, a reported cat abduction, and a new one with the woman who had the issue with the pickles. She had gone back to the Burger King that she said had ripped her off, and they were now refusing to serve her.

Travis agreed to swing by and check each call off in turn and then file the reports after he returned to the office. But first, he had to drive all the way back to return Maggie to the car she'd left parked near the substation.

Maggie Fisk had told him on the way out of the clubhouse that she planned to return to Florida Tech and return the following day with a search team that would scour the marshlands looking for the giant crocodile. She had also reluctantly agreed to let the matter of closing the entire golf course drop. In return, she would be allowed back with her team to investigate further, but they would not be permitted to interfere at all with the preparations for the upcoming tournament. That had been made abundantly clear, by an irritated Atticus Goulding when they had returned to ask for permission.

Maggie now sat in the passenger seat with one arm propped on the armrest to her right and her head resting in her palm.

For the first time since he'd met her, she was not talking. He actually sort of missed her strong will and stream of big words, at least when compared to the prospects of going out on the lousy calls he had ahead of him. But, on balance, he'd also get to meet the crazy woman who had complained about the pickles, and that might make for a good story to tell later when he got home to his wife. He also had the report on Mr. Robertson that needed to be closed and filed before the day was over. *Heart attack*, he had decided would be the reported cause. Even if it was foul play that had been the actual reason for the man's death, with the constant roadblocks he'd faced over investigating it, there was no way it could be reported as anything else—if he wanted to keep his job, that was. And, right now, he wanted to keep that job. He had nothing else.

He put the key in the ignition and turned it to start the engine. Then, right before he put the SUV in gear, he noticed a man running from the side of the clubhouse. The guy hopped in a golf cart and went speeding off. Travis shook his head to clear it and dropped the gearshift into D for drive. He eased off the gas then suddenly slammed his foot down hard on the brake pedal.

Both he and Maggie jerked forward. She slapped her hands on the dashboard as she was pulled tight against her restraints.

Another man rolled off the front of the Interceptor and continued racing for another golf cart. The guy was dressed in dark blue with white and red medical insignias on his uniform. He had a large black bag hung over one shoulder, and he tossed that bag into a golf cart and went tearing out of the parking lot like a bat out of Hell.

"Something's not right," Maggie said, stating the obvious.

Travis felt a big sinking feeling drop his stomach a metaphorical ten feet. He knew what had happened the instant before his phone rang. Hurriedly, he answered the call. Ms. Scott was on the other end.

"Travis, I just got a 911 call routed to our station. They couldn't raise you on the radio, so I figured your phone might work. I sure hope you haven't left Clear Creek yet, honey. Something terrible has happened. Lord have mercy. It's—"

"Alligator attack?" he asked.

There was a pause on the line, then Ms. Scott said, *"How in the world did you know that?"*

TWENTY

ATTACK

TRAVIS GUNNED THE engine on the Interceptor and tore out after the golf cart, not wanting it to get behind the building where he might lose sight of it. He clicked on the light bar and maneuvered onto the narrow asphalt path leading away from the clubhouse and out onto the golf course. As he drove past carts filled with golfers, they turned to watch him go by, shock and amazement painting their faces as if they were not sure what was going on, but knew it couldn't be good.

When he topped a rise and began to descend back down the other side, Travis saw a mass of people surrounding the edge of the swamp. The golf cart ahead of them came to a stop, and the man dressed in blue jumped out and just stood there a moment, assessing the scene. He raised a two-way radio and said something into it.

Travis stopped the SUV and jumped out, scanning the area for any still-lingering danger and to see if anyone had taken charge yet. No one had.

There was an overturned golf cart near the water's edge and a crowd of people all spread out around it. Travis followed the man in blue as the guy weaved through the crowd, hoping that the guy knew more about what was going on than he did.

The crowd parted to let Travis through, and near the water, sitting next to the overturned golf cart was a man and a young boy. The man was comforting the young boy. Travis recognized the kid, but not the man. It was the younger of the two brothers he had met earlier. The medic dressed in blue was already kneeling and examining the boy for injuries.

"What happened here?" Travis said to someone in the crowd as he approached. His eyes roamed looking for someone who would speak up. It was then that he noticed that a large amount of blood covered the grass, and there were furrows in the mud that led back to the water's edge. He traced those tracks all the way back to the kid by the golf cart with his gaze.

The kid was wrapped in a white windbreaker, but it was evident what had happened. There was blood all over him. His sandy brown hair was matted down against his scalp, and his face was streaked with splashes of dark red blood and brown mud.

Travis dropped to one knee and checked the child over himself, glancing once at the medic who gave him a curt nod. The kid appeared uninjured, so Travis nodded back at the medic and the man sitting on the ground next to the kid and stood back up.

He raised his voice and said to those around him, "Can anyone here tell me what happened?"

The chattering around him died down for a brief moment then everyone seemed to want to speak at once.

"Gator," one guy said.

"Huge. It was—" a kid was saying, eyes wide.

"Saw it go that way," said another man, pointing off into the marsh.

"It got him," said someone else from behind Travis. He whirled, and there was a teenage boy who appeared shaken up and was now moving stiffly and slowly.

Travis put a hand on the teen's shoulder and asked, "What happened, son?"

"This," the teen said, raising his phone in a shaky hand and tapping the screen.

A video began to play. Maggie sidled up next to him. She leaned closer to watch the video. In the shaky video, he could clearly see the overturned golf cart. Then the image panned quickly, and Travis saw a flash of something that at first he couldn't believe. His mind reeled, taking it all in. The sound on the video was high pitched and tinny, but he could make out the obvious signs of distress.

Holy hell, he thought. *It's Huge. Giant. What the heck is—?*

It was an alligator, or crocodile, and it was snapping at a man who was standing in front of it. The gigantic jaws were opening and closing, and the head was pivoting back and forth.

"It's twisting to see in front of it," Maggie commented.

The camera panned a little more, and Travis noticed a smallish shape on the ground near one of the creature's large front feet or claws or whatever they were called. The image refocused, and Travis was certain now of what he saw. It was one of the two kids he had met earlier, the older of the brothers. The kid wasn't moving and was splayed face down in the mud.

The father was trying to coax the alligator away from the kid, waving a towel at it, taunting it. The giant crocodile kept turning its head and opening and closing its jaws, but it would not take the bait and come after the man, so the father rounded the giant crocodile to the other side, working his way ever closer to his unmoving son.

Travis's heart sank in his chest, knowing what was about to happen and not being able to prevent it. In the horrifying scene, he could see his own son in the young kid and him as the desperate father trying to save him. Travis would have done the same thing, whatever it took, anything at all. His mind rooted hard for the father, wanting him to win and be able to free his son. He didn't want to believe the alternative. It was almost too terrifying to contemplate.

He continued to watch in abject horror as the father made one more desperate lunge to get to his son and grab the kid by the hand.

Then the man misstepped and slipped and fell in the mud.

The giant crocodile swung its head around and crashed the long snout down on the man, who was now digging trenches in the soft earth trying to push away from it and escape his inevitable death. The father had been pinned down when the head had landed on top of him, but he somehow twisted and squirmed free. And it was now obvious by the way one of the man's arms was hanging that it had broken, perhaps been crushed. With his remaining good arm, he grabbed his son by the hand and attempted to drag him alongside.

The crocodile squirmed sideways again and the mighty head twisted and the mouth opened and rolled the man sideways. The jaws then snapped closed in the blink of an eye, trapping the father in a death grip. The crocodile held him there for a moment while the struggling man pounded on the things head, mouth spraying and spitting blood. And then slowly, with the squirming man clamped firmly between its jaws, the crocodile retreated into the marsh.

Travis wanted to be sick. Nothing he had ever been through had prepared him for such a horror. Movies, books, television. Nothing compared to seeing it happen for real and knowing that a man had just paid the ultimate price trying to save his son. Everything around Travis went out of focus, and his entire body tingled with empathetic fear. He thought for a second that he might pass out.

Then he felt a squeeze on his bicep. It was Maggie.

As the world around him came back into focus and sounds became more than a blur of noises, he heard more accusations coming from the golfers.

"Why is this golf course still open?" said one man.

Another father had his two sons at his side, holding them both tight. Travis focused on the man, sharing in the relief.

"Someone needs to shoot that goddamned thing," another man said, making a fist in front of him.

"What are you going to do about this, Sheriff?" another said. It was a guy in a spotless white golf shirt and checkered pants. "This place is way too dangerous. It's...It's...I'm going to sue the crap out of—"

"They'll be no suing, Mr. Jackson," Atticus Goulding said, coming up from behind Travis. "This was just an unfortunate and tragic accident. Wasn't it, Deputy?"

Travis said nothing. He ignored the men and went to the young boy again. He kneeled down in front of him. The little boy was clearly still in shock. He wasn't even crying.

"I'm sorry," Travis said, drawing a series of deep breaths.

The little boy looked him straight in the eyes and said, "You told me no gators were going to come get us…"

TWENTY ONE

FULL STEAM AHEAD

"YES, SIR," TRAVIS said sternly. "I'll take care of it. Thank you, sir."

The line went dead. Travis looked back over the dwindling crowd as they began dispersing. The ambulance had arrived an hour earlier and had taken the poor, shaken boy off to the hospital for further examination. There were no external injuries on him, but the internal ones, Travis knew, would take a lifetime to heal, if they ever did heal at all. He could hardly imagine what that kid was going through now, losing both his father and his older brother in such a horrific way. If the situation were reversed, and it had been his son that had been killed? Travis didn't even want to consider it. Not for a second.

The phone call had been with his boss, the county sheriff, and Travis was told in no uncertain terms that he was to personally handle the situation with the attack and organize the response in the aftermath. Even the paperwork necessities were being temporarily suspended as an accommodation, and the sheriff was sending down an additional team of department resources to assist with the investigation, but it would be up to Travis to allocate those resources appropriately, at least for the next few hours. The sheriff himself planned to come and join them as soon as he met with the boy's mother and had a chance to hold a press conference to mollify the media before they descended into their own feeding frenzy. Travis was not to let any of the media outlets onto the golf course under any circumstances, nor was he to shut down the upcoming golf tournament. There were just too many important people coming—Hollywood celebrities, sports stars, music people, and even a few high-ranking government officials. It was now on Travis alone to ensure their total and complete safety, and he was to work in concert with Atticus Goulding and do whatever the man deemed necessary to make the golf course safe and secure for the event.

Fuck that, was all Travis could think of. He had other ideas.

While he had wanted to tell his boss his suspicions, he was feeling the crushing influence of what he'd always called "the good old boy's network." And, without evidence to back his theories up, he would just be pissing in the wind and getting that piss all over himself.

Though, through much of the call, he had been teetering on the edge of just not caring and blurting it out. And, in addition, he had been so angry that he had almost quit on the spot and walked away.

But he couldn't just walk away. He didn't know why. He just couldn't. Not now. Not when he had been—

He let it drop and took a series of deep breaths.

"What did he say?" Maggie asked when he returned to her.

"The tournament goes on as scheduled."

She huffed loudly and looked back at him as if she could barely repress her anger. "Seriously? You have to close the course. There is no other choice. You just have to. Do you understand? This is not a joke. That thing is something I have never seen before. We need to study it, and to do that we need to make sure that no one else gets hurt. Otherwise—"

"If I did that," he said, "I'd be replaced in a heartbeat. That man holds all the cards." He nodded toward Atticus Goulding. "There is no way for me to stop any of this without losing my job. And if I did lose my job, they'd bring in someone else, and none of that would change a damn thing. The course would stay open."

She grumbled and wiped the sweat around her glasses with her fingers and flicked it away. "As soon as word leaks out on this, every two-bit, red-necked alligator hunter in the state will be here trying to kill it. We can't let that happen. This animal is unique. It might only be a freak of nature, but that doesn't mean we should destroy it without taking the opportunity to study it first."

"It's already killed three people that we know of. There could be more. We have to find it, and we have to kill it."

"No," she said. "You can't. It's too important. You have to close the golf course down now and let us study it. I've already contacted Dr. Galen. He's taking the first flight back and will be assembling a research team. At least give us a few days to locate it. Delay this stupid golf tournament. They are just a waste of time. Shut it all down and keep the people safe."

"I can't do that."

"Then there is going to be a bloodbath," she said, turning away from him.

Through clenched teeth, he uttered, "Not if we kill that damn gator, crocodile, or whatever the hell it is first."

"No," she snapped. "And if you dare to go after it and kill it... How in the world do you plan to do *that*?"

"By any means necessary," he said.

TWENTY TWO

ANY MEANS NECESSARY

ANY MEANS NECESSARY turned out to be a broken-down drunk by the name of Ely Beauregard Stone. Ms. Scott had given Travis the address and told him that if anyone knew anything about gators, it was crazy old Ely Stone. He'd killed more alligators than Colonel Sanders had killed chickens. Though, Travis was fairly certain the last bit had mostly been an exaggeration on her part. But when he drove onto Ely's property, it became pretty clear that she was not too far off the mark.

Broken down cars and rusting appliances littered the front yard. Sitting on poles and hanging from dangling wire lines were alligator skulls of all sizes. Desiccated skins were stretched out and drying on racks in the sun. Old metal wheels and potbelly stoves and galvanized basins filled with brackish water lined the broken concrete path leading to the front porch. Behind all that was a house with peeling paint that looked as though a stiff breeze could blow it down.

Travis closed the door on the SUV, and Maggie Fisk came around to join him.

"You can't possibly be serious," she said. "Look at all those skulls. This guy is a killer, not a hunter. A hunter would—"

"We don't need a hunter," he said. "We need a killer. Wait by the car, please. I'll be right back."

Travis opened a waist-high gate in the short chain link fence that surrounded the property and stepped through it and onto the crumbling concrete walkway.

"That's far enough," a voice said.

Travis froze.

A tall, rail-thin man with a long gray beard and wild, wiry hair came out from under the eaves of the house. He was dressed in a stained wife-beater tank top and was brandishing a weapon. On closer examination, Travis realized the weapon wasn't a gun. It was a crossbow with a large scope on it and a gleaming broadhead arrow, ready to fire, which made the weapon just as lethal as a gun, if not more so.

Travis raised his hands shoulder high. "I'm looking for Ely."

"Who is ya that's lookin'?" the grizzled man called back.

"The town's new deputy, Travis Morrison, sir."

"I ain't done nothin' wrong. Where's the old deputy?"

"Are you Ely? Ely Stone?"

"What if I is?"

"Then I would want to talk with you."

"I told ya. I ain't done nuthin' wrong. That young punk had it coming."

Travis ran it back in his mind and connected the dots.

"No, it isn't about that. I'm not here to arrest you."

The crossbow came up a little higher. "Then what are you here for?"

"You were a Marine, right?"

"Semper Fi. What's it to ya?"

"My dad was a Marine. Second Battalion, Fourth Marines."

The crossbow lowered a bit. "The Magnificent Bastards?"

It took a brief second for Travis to process before he tried on Ely's accent and answered, "Yeah, that's exactly what my daddy was."

"What'd 'bout you? You serve, boy?"

"Never had the pleasure, but I would have been a Marine if I had served. I can tell you that."

The crossbow lowered fully and Ely tilted his head back, which Travis took for an invitation to start moving again. He lowered his arms and weaved between the various debris littering the front yard. When he got to the porch, the old man backed himself into a hanging seat, still holding the crossbow but lowering it to his lap. Travis sat in a wicker chair directly across from him.

"Drink?" Ely offered, holding out a mason jar filled with clear liquid.

"Can't," Travis said.

"Bullshit, son. You come here to talk to me, that means ya drink with me, too."

Travis rose and accepted the mason jar. He sniffed the contents. It was moonshine, all right. Or at least he was fairly certain it was since he'd never actually tasted it before.

"Made it myself," Ely admitted as a challenge. "So it's good and fresh."

Travis let the obvious bending of the law pass right on by him. Instead, he steeled himself for what he figured would be the most awful thing he had ever tasted. He sipped from the jar. Then he pulled the mason jar away and held it up to the light and stared through it, lowered it and tasted it again.

"How?" he asked in utter amazement. He'd tried just about every other type of hard liquor there was—tequila, whiskey, vodka, gin, rum, and brandy. All of them had distinct flavors. Many of them didn't taste all that good unless they were very expensive. But this? This was the first time he'd tried high-proof alcohol that was so smooth. It burned a little, but it was one of the most remarkable things he'd ever consumed. He could drink it almost like water. But that would be bad, so he let the taste of the second sip be enough to sustain him.

"Secret's in usin' ground gator livers in the mash," Ely said with a wink. "Cleans up the impurities."

Whatever the hell it was that was used, Travis figured he could easily get used to drinking something that smooth. He wanted to take another sip, but handed the jar back instead.

Ely stared crosswise at him. "So yer daddy was a Marine, huh?"

"Yes," Travis replied. "Where did you serve, if I may ask?"

"Ya may... Where didn't I serve. From Chu Lai to Ca Lu to Saigon on the way out. We lost a lot of good men there thanks to all them commie-lovers back home." He raised the jar in salute to the dead and drank deeply. "So yer daddy was two-four then? Magnificent Bastards... Good folk."

"He was," Travis said, replying to the "Magnificent Bastards" part. His father had done his best to live up to the namesake of the outfit, and Travis had the emotional bruises to prove it.

"I was with Echo Company, myself," Ely said. "So, what's cha you doing here, boy? Is it all about that Army brat I gave a little spankin' to?"

"No, I have something else to talk to you about." Travis drew a deep breath. "Have you heard yet about the alligator attack out at Clearwater Creek Golf Course?"

Ely stopped swinging. "Nope, go on."

Travis filled Ely in on both the supposed heart attack of Harold Robertson—to which he didn't seem to mind—and the attack on the father and son—which caused him to tug at his beard and frown.

When Travis finished, Ely said, "Gators don't normally attack people like that. If them damn commies would let me hunt 'em year round, we'd have a lot less of 'em bothering them rich polyester-wearing sacks of shit. Sorry about the little kid and the dad. They'alls in a better place now."

"This is no ordinary alligator we are dealing with here. That's why I came to you. Beatrice Scott recommended I talk with you first. Said you were the best hunter in the county."

"Best in the state," he said proudly, slapping his hand on his chest. "Old Bee...she's a good church-going woman, praise Jesus Lord."

Travis nodded. "And according to a marine biologist I brought in to help with the initial investigation, this is a crocodile we are dealing with. A very large one at that."

"Crocodile? That's bullshit, boy. Ain't no crocodiles this far inland. They's live out near the beaches, getting fat on tourists dumb enough to feed 'em. Don't need no ma-rineen bi-o-lo-gist telling me 'bout crocs being this far from the ocean."

"I honestly don't know the difference," Travis said. "That's why I'm here."

"I tells you that it being a croc is complete bullshit."

Travis dug his phone out of his pocket. He pulled up the video that he'd been sent of the attack, started it, and handed the phone over to Ely.

While Ely watched, the sound playing from the tiny speaker was disturbing enough that Travis relived the video in his mind. His heart beat faster and his breathing shallowed, and he became lightheaded again, and that lightheadedness wasn't just from the two sips of moonshine.

Ely held the phone out at arm's length and watched the entire thing without comment. When the video ended, he handed the phone back and drew a deep breath.

Travis swallowed thickly, then asked, "Do you think you can help us hunt this thing down?"

Ely raised the mason jar in a toast but did not take another drink. "Ya, I can. Sumthin' like that you don't see every day." He wiped at the corner of his eye then raised the mason jar higher and said, "Let's go kill us a big-ass croc."

TWENTY THREE

DINNER BREAK

TRAVIS BIT INTO his burger and started chewing. Before he was even finished, he grabbed a pair of fries from the cardboard container in front of him, dredged them through a pool of ketchup, and added them to those already in his mouth. Across the picnic table from him sat Maggie Fisk. She was picking at a salad in a plastic container, but not really eating it. The sun had gone down, but the night was still swelteringly hot, and the bugs swarming around the overhead lights in front of Ed's Burgers were buzzing loud enough that both he and Maggie had to raise their voices a bit to be heard. Off behind them, a bug zapper kept going off, crackling and popping and sizzling every time an insect ran into the wire mesh and died a smoky death.

Ely Stone had gone off to pick up his boat from his cousin's storage lot to get it ready for the night's adventures, and they were to meet him around nine p.m. near the launch and get started with the hunt there. He said they could work their way back behind the golf course and stay in deeper water, right where he swore any big gator or croc would want to call home.

Maggie swatted at a mosquito that had landed on her arm. "I'm against all this, so you know. We shouldn't even be hunting that crocodile. We should be studying it. But you don't want to do that, do you? It'll only be two days until Dr. Galen arrives, so why can't we just hold off until then?"

"You want me to tell that to the mother who lost her husband and son?" Travis said, wiping his mouth on a paper napkin.

"Of course not. But it isn't right killing something we know so little about. We are the ones invading their territory. Don't they have the same right to exist that we do?"

"Not if it has killed someone and still presents such a dangerous threat. It's an alligator, not a person. So the laws don't apply the same way."

"That doesn't make it right to just go kill it. That's thinking two wrongs make a right."

He said nothing for several seconds, then, "The sheriff will be here tomorrow with his cameras and his media circus. If we don't have something to show for tonight's activities, then it will be my ass that gets handed over to the press."

"You are so overly concerned about losing your job that you are willing to kill a magnificent creature...?"

He said nothing and took another bite, suppressing his anger. It wasn't only about his job. And even if it were, the press would have a field day with him, that's for sure. Shooting an unarmed kid back in Oregon, then trying to escape by moving to Florida and then being responsible for not maintaining the safety of the town he was sworn to protect and allowing a father and son to be attacked by a giant crocodile...?

They would gut him like a fish.

"Think of what that crocodile might be," she said. "What I saw in those pictures and video was no simple crocodile. No, not at all. I think it might represent something we may have never seen before. Or maybe even something that we thought had gone extinct long ago. We can't possibly kill it. That would be a terrible abuse of nature." She shook her head. "No, we can't kill it. Not until we understand what it is first, and then only if we have no other choice."

He pointed at her with a long, dangling french fry. "When you went alone into the swamp, didn't you bring a gun along with you?"

"Yes, but that's different. That gun was for my protection only. For self-defense."

"It was a .44 Magnum," he said, emphasizing his point by shaking the dangling french fry and dipping his head toward her. "That's a damn big gun."

She picked again at her salad.

He set his burger down and sipped from his soda. "I mean, come on, think about it. Even if this thing is a once in a lifetime opportunity, it has to be stopped before it can hurt anyone again. And you saw the size of it. Is there any way you can think of that we can capture that thing and not have to shoot it first?"

"There is."

"By tomorrow morning?"

She paused. "If it is your job you are concerned about..."

"It's not only my job..." He let it hang there and went back to nibbling on his french fries.

"Then what is it?"

He leaned closer, considering whether to tell her or not.

"What?" she asked again.

"When I saw that video, I saw my own son lying there in the mud and me struggling to save him. I saw him being attacked by that goddamned monster. I'm sorry, but it just has to die."

"Then this is about revenge?" she asked, leaning back and dropping her fork into her salad bowl.

"You can call it that if you want, but this is about ending the threat of that thing once and for all."

She exhaled, loudly. "I can't be a part of this any longer. If you want to go hunt it down and kill it, you can do so without me. I still say it's wrong."

"I'd rather have you come along with us," he said. "You know far more about these things than I do. But there is no question about it. We will kill it as soon as we find it. And then you can study it to your heart's content."

She grabbed her fork and poked at her salad again. Finally, without taking another bite, she threw the fork down and climbed out from the picnic bench. She swatted at the swarming gnats and mosquitos that had gathered in front of her face and took a step back.

"I can't help you with this. I won't be a party to killing such a magnificent creature."

She began to walk away. He opened his mouth to say something, then realized there was nothing he could really say that would change her mind. He picked up his soda and rattled the ice inside, and took one last gurgling sip.

TWENTY FOUR

BIGGER BOAT

"YOU'RE GOING TO need a bigger boat," Travis said as he looked over the tiny skiff that Ely had tied up against the small dock near the boat launch. And then he remembered where he'd heard that line before and shuddered a bit, wondering if his experience was going to be the same as that damn movie that had scared the crap out of him when he was a little kid. After seeing it, he hadn't wanted to go near the ocean until he was well over eighteen. He just knew there was some shark that would be lurking under the surface and would come and get him if he ever did go in the ocean. It was also on his mind when he had gone swimming in lakes, even though he knew the ridiculousness of that fear.

"Boat's big enough," Ely said, hoisting a red can of gasoline and connecting it up to an ancient outboard motor that was missing its cover.

Under the glare of a single sodium lamp at the end of the dock, the dull aluminum hull of the boat appeared to have been made in the seventies, maybe the sixties. There was a single seat at the bow end, and a small wheel on a podium halfway back and to the starboard side. The boat had so many dents and dings in it that Travis wondered if the hull was even sound and seaworthy, or marsh-worthy, or whatever the term would be in this situation. Two oversized fishing rods with spin-cast reels rested against a rear bench seat, as well as a large gaffing stick and the crossbow Travis had seen Ely with earlier. There wasn't anything else in the boat other than various ropes, nets, and some scuffed-up red and white buoys set next to a pair of old plastic coolers.

Travis patted the relatively small 9mm at his hip, realizing the inadequacy of it in this situation. He had been issued a shotgun, but he hadn't bothered to bring it along with him, and the drive back to go fetch it might take an hour or more. But as he scanned the boat, that hour-long drive was starting to make a whole lot of sense right now.

"You do know how big that crocodile was?" he asked.

"Biggest damn one I'd ever seen," Ely said. "Shouldn't be no problem, though. We don't have to drag her in the boat, jus' shoot 'er and tie her up alongside."

"Her?"

"That's a she if I ever seen one."

"How can you tell?"

"I just can," he said and spat over the side.

Travis let the matter drop. "Don't you have any guns onboard?"

Ely started laughing and slapping his thigh. "They don't let me have no guns no more. Say's I'm too dangerous with 'em. I got this beaut, though." He scooted forward and picked up the crossbow. "This is better for gators anyway. Makes a bigger hole for the blood to come spurtin' out."

"Lifejackets?"

"What'd you need one of them for? With all them gators in the water, one of them just makes you bob about while they 'et at ya from below."

Travis had a very bad feeling about all this, suddenly wishing he had not chosen to come along. Maybe Maggie had been right. Maybe this gator was just too much to take on without getting more people involved.

He pulled out his cell phone and texted his wife a single message: I LOVE YOU. His thumb hovered over the SEND button, then he pressed it, hoping it wasn't the last message he ever sent her.

Right away she texted back: WTF? WHAT'S WRONG?

Him: NOTHING. EVERYTHING'S OK.

Her: SURE?

Him: YES. FINE. HOME LATE.

She ended with: LOVE YOU TOO. BE SAFE.

Putting away the phone, he pulled on the headlamp that he'd been told to bring along and checked to make sure it worked. Wherever he turned his head, he saw the light beam, and it made the blackish water appear green wherever the beam landed, and all the bugs floating in the air looked like motes of dust. He glanced over at Ely.

"Get that damn thing outta my face," the old guy said, hands going up to block the glare. "You're blinding me with that. Don't go pointing that at me again, hear?" He shuffled to the steering podium and turned an old key on a dangling chain, then returned to the engine, wrapped a rope around a wheel at the top and yanked. Then he repeated the process. And again.

With a sputtering cough, the old engine caught on the third try and began belching a cloud of exhaust. Ely returned to the steering podium and played with the throttle until the engine was purring away, or at least thumping.

The cloud of exhaust kept growing and soon Travis was forced to wave the noxious smoke out from in front of his face. He moved to get out of the advancing cloud and glanced down into the boat, then back at his parked vehicle at the top of the boat ramp.

"Best we get going now, hear?" Ely said.

Travis sighed and stepped onto the boat.

TWENTY FIVE

GATOR FISHING

TRAVIS HAD ALMOST nodded off when his phone began to buzz. Scrambling in the darkness for it, he answered and held it to one ear.

"Deputy Morrison, this is Atticus Goulding. I am calling to check up on the results of your search tonight. Have you managed to find and kill that crocodile yet?"

Blinking himself fully awake, Travis first wondered where in the hell Atticus had gotten his phone number, and why he had called.

"Not yet," he said, slightly stupefied by the surprise call.

"I am expecting results. Do you understand me? I spoke with the sheriff earlier tonight, and he has assured me that you would take care of the matter before we open for business tomorrow. There is no way in hell we will be delaying the tournament or closing the course. There are just too many issues to—" He stopped talking, and Travis heard him take a breath. *"You just need to get this done and done quickly. Are we clear?"*

"Yes," Travis said, hesitantly, wondering what would happen if he said "no."

"That did not sound very reassuring."

"Yes, sir. We'll get it done tonight." Inside, he deflated. Much as he wanted to tell this man to go straight to Hell and not pass Go, he couldn't bring himself to do so. Not when he thought of his wife and son at home counting on him. This man could end his career quickly with another call to the sheriff.

"Good," Atticus said. *"That's better. What I expected. When this is all over, son, you can ask me for anything. A free club membership...anything. We are all counting on you."*

The phone call disconnected, leaving Travis puzzled by the last part of the conversation. It had sounded almost conciliatory. Then, thinking off all he had to do, he stared back at the dark form of Ely a couple of feet away and wondered how that skinny old man was going to help kill the biggest monster he'd ever seen.

The silvery moonlight reflected off the black water like a mirror. Off in the background, the frogs and insects created a cacophony of noises that were almost deafening in their intensity.

"Why hunt them at night?" Travis asked, wanting to speak so he would not fall back into a stupor.

"Night's best, 'cuz that's when gators like to feed. You just keep watching the water, son. That big thing's out here, I can tell you. Ain't seen no other gators in hours, which tells me they all scared a sumthin'."

Travis checked his watch—3:42 a.m. Sunrise would be in a few hours and they still had nothing to show for their night on the water. He yawned and glanced at the two fishing poles in their holders while Ely got up and went to the first of the poles and started to reel it back in. When the hook came up, all that was there was a shiny piece of metal that gleamed in the moonlight.

"See there," Ely said. "Gators 'et the bait."

And almost as soon as he had said that, something bumped against the boat, rocking it slightly.

"Get me some more," Ely whispered.

Travis wrinkled his nose in anticipation and opened the first of the coolers set between them, then remembered it wasn't the right one. But before he closed the lid, he took note of what was inside—long red sticks that looked like road flares. Then he checked closer. Those weren't road flares, they were dynamite. He reached for one of the dark red sticks and drew it out carefully. There was a short fuse stuck in one end.

"Whoa there, sonny. Best leave those alone."

"What the hell?" Travis said.

"They's more for fishing, or when I gets a bit lazy."

"Do you have a license for this?" Travis said in awe, holding up the single stick of dynamite and examining it.

"License? Who says I needs one of those? Git that bait on the hook, boy. We ain't got all night."

Travis set the dynamite back in the cooler and closed the lid. In all his years in law enforcement, which hadn't been many, he had never before handled dynamite, much less had seen it. Now there was enough sitting a few feet away from him that he was certain would blow them into a fine pink mist if it ever went off. And it was then he began to seriously question the sanity of this endeavor. Out on a small boat, in the dark, with a crazy person, and trying to hunt down a man-eating crocodile—with a cooler filled with dynamite. Long shivers raced up and down his spine. He suddenly wanted to be somewhere else. Anywhere else.

"Git another fish head on there," Ely said, this time with more insistence.

Trembling with a newly realized fear, Travis reached inside the second cooler and brought out a decaying, putrefied fish head. Holding his breath and leaning forward, he grabbed the line and strung the hook through the gills just like Ely had demonstrated earlier. Ely then nodded his approval and did a slow cast out over the side of the boat. The baited hook splashed in the dark water, sank below the surface, and all noises from the cast faded into the background hum of nature.

"We've been at this for hours," Travis said. "And there's been nothing to show for it. Should we go find another spot? There doesn't seem to be anything here."

"Shhh," Ely whispered above the ambient noise. "They's here. Jus' keep yerself quiet and they'all shows up."

Shaking his head, Travis reached over the side of the boat to wash his hands in the somewhat cooler water.

And he saw it a half-second before it came bursting out of the water at him. A pair of snapping jaws rocketed straight at him. The gator crested the surface and, fortunately, going on pure instinct, Travis drew back, and the alligator's jaws clamped shut right where his hands had been, and the water splashed and frothed.

Travis then fell back on his ass inside the boat and set it to rocking.

"Almost got you," Ely observed. "Gotta be more careful there, son." He went back to reeling the second line in slowly.

Panting heavily, Travis reoriented himself and climbed back into the seat. He let out a long breath and tried to still his rapidly beating heart.

"Why didn't you warn me they could do that?"

"You di-n't ask, son."

Head twisting back and forth, Travis said, "If there are gators here, then doesn't that blow your theory about that big one being nearby? Should we move somewhere else now?"

Ely reeled in a little more, and then jerked the pole. The fiberglass rod bent nearly to the water, and Ely went with it, standing up and leaning over the side. But he dug in his heels and held on. The line started playing out from the reel with a buzzing noise. Travis came alongside as Ely regained his seat on the bow and clipped the rod and reel to a strap affixed to his seat.

"What can I do?" Travis asked.

"Nuthin' yet," Ely said. He pulled on the rod and started reeling in the line. Then he let off, and the line went back out. "Get my crossbow," he said.

Travis did what he was asked. He raised the crossbow, feeling the weight of it and testing his vision through the scope while Ely pulled on the rod and reeled in some more line.

"Soon as this sum'bitch breaches, you go 'n shoot it. Put a shot right behind its front legs. Straight in its lungs."

Ely kept pulling and reeling. Travis clicked on his headlamp and scanned the water. He saw the fishing line making Z patterns on the surface and shaking about as the boat slowly began to pivot around on the anchor line. He raised the crossbow to his shoulder but couldn't hold it steady. He also couldn't see squat through the scope. He lowered it and double-checked that he would be clear of the steel line attached the to the crossbow bolt, then raised the crossbow again to his shoulder and prepared to fire.

The alligator surfaced and rolled onto one side, giving him an almost perfect shot at its underbelly. Even though it was difficult to make out, he guess at it and centered the shot in the scope the best he could, and squeezed the trigger. The bolt shot out of the crossbow as the recoil pushed back hard against his shoulder.

The shot went wild and missed. Harmlessly, it hit the water just over the alligator's back and created a tiny splash as the steel line played out behind it.

"Dammit," Ely said, "can't you shoot for shit?"

"This isn't even the alligator—crocodile—we wanted," Travis barked back.

"Don't matter none. Gator's hooked, so it's good as dead now. Load dat up and try again."

Travis pulled another crossbow bolt off the quiver, set it beside himself, and stood up to draw the bow. He put his foot through the front stirrup and pinned it against the bottom of the boat and pulled back.

The gator bumped against the boat and set it to rocking. Trying to stabilize himself, Travis tripped over his own feet and fell sideways. His back foot caught on a loop of rope, and windmilling backward, he toppled over the side of the boat and splashed in the water and sank below the surface.

Frantically, he flapped his arms and clawed for the surface. Something bumped up against his right leg. He kicked at whatever it was and threw an arm up and over the side of the boat in near panic. He managed to get that arm up over the side when he was bumped again and fell back into the water.

With surprising clarity, he could picture an entire group of alligators below him, all opening their jaws, getting ready to take big chunks out of his thrashing legs. He kicked again with all his might and broke the surface and slapped a hand over the side of the boat.

But it wasn't helping. Without something for his feet to stand on, he couldn't get enough purchase to climb or pull himself any higher. The boat was tilting further and further, with the edge nearest him getting dangerously close to the water.

Fuel by an icy fear, he kicked his legs together with all his might, feeling them move sluggishly underwater.

It was barely enough.

And just as he started to pull himself up the side of the boat, a hand landed on his back, gripped his shirt, and practically jerked him from the water. Still kicking, he was able to get his shoulders higher than the boat's edge and locked it under his armpits. He swung one leg up, caught the side, then swung up the other.

Finally, like a fish dragged from a net, he rolled over onto his side and plopped down inside the boat and twisted until he was on his back, panting furiously at the stars speckling the blackness above.

"Goddammit, son. You cost me a good rod and reel," Ely spat.

Upside down, Travis stared back at the man as he spun around and prepared to sit up. He blinked a few times and realized the head-mounted lamp that was once on his head was now missing. He clawed his way to a seated position and glanced over the side of the boat. He could see where his headlamp had landed in the murky water. It was glowing from somewhere deep below the surface. Soaking wet, he shoved himself back up and into his seat, still breathing hard.

"Here, drink this," Ely said. "It'll get the taste of swamp outta yer mouth."

Not paying any attention to what he'd been given, he tipped back the jar and gulped deeply from it and kept going until he'd drained the entire thing. Then he felt the smooth burn and realized what he'd just done. He'd consumed almost an entire mason jar filled with moonshine.

"Guess we ain't getting no gators or no crocs tonight," Ely said, chuckling softly. "Damn shame. But I suspect it won't matter to you much anyway…"

TWENTY SIX

STUMBLING

BACK AT THE boat ramp parking lot, still soaked to the bone, Travis stumbled up the sloped concrete ramp to his Ford Interceptor, feet slipping and sliding on the slimy surface. He was still far too drunk to drive, and the rising sun meant that sleeping it off inside the vehicle was going to present a problem that even his cloudy mind could make sense of. He'd be smothered by the day's heat if he shut himself inside. So, instead of facing the prospects of being baked to death in the SUV oven, he figured to call his wife and have her come pick him up. It would be far better to have her kill him for his stupidity than die from the heat. But as he fumbled for his keys, he spotted a lone figure sitting on a park bench, watching him as he tried to make his way across the parking lot without falling on his ass.

"Didn't get it, did you?" Maggie Fisk said as she hopped off the bench to come join him.

He shook his head slowly, numbly.

"Hey, are you okay?"

He waved her off. No, he was not okay. He had come up empty handed in his search for the giant alligator, or crocodile, or whatever the hell it was. Plus, he was more intoxicated now than he'd ever been in his entire life. He could barely walk and could only shamble forward like a zombie.

She waited for him to get closer. "I figured you two wouldn't find it. A specimen like that doesn't want to be found. It has to be very old, and very wise. How do you think it got so big in the first place?"

He shook his head and mumbled something, but didn't even know himself what he had said.

"You really look like shit. You know that? Long night?"

He clamped his eyes shut to keep the world from tilting sideways, then blinked them open again. His stomach was gurgling and he wanted to be sick. He belched into a fist.

She came up alongside him and stopped short, waving a hand in front of her face. "You're not injured, you're drunk! And you really stink like that swamp. You know it is not smart to get in the water with all those alligators and snakes, right?" She let out a short, sharp chuckle.

He took another few steps toward the park bench she had vacated, and while trying to clear the curb between the asphalt and the grassy area surrounding the bench, he tripped and fell forward, landing hard in the dirt and grass. He stayed there like a knocked-out fighter down for the count.

"You really aren't okay, are you?"

He heard another voice say, "Man needs ta learn how ta hold his liquor." It was Ely.

Travis remained in the horizontal position, though he rolled his head to one side to keep the sun out of his eyes.

"What happened out there?" Maggie asked.

"Who you?" Ely barked.

"I'm Maggie. Didn't he tell you about me?"

"Saw you with him earlier. You's that ma-rineen bi-o-lo-gist into gators?"

"That would be me. You didn't find it, did you?"

"No, lill' girlie, we di'nt. Had us a nice gator hooked, though. Then, 'stead of shootin' it, that dumbass fool decided to jump in and go swimming around a bit. Lost me some good gear when it happened."

Travis groaned.

"Is he going to die?" Maggie asked.

"He's just had a bit too much to drink, is all."

"You were drinking while hunting?" she asked, incredulous.

"Wouldn't have it any other way," Ely said, gave a quick laugh, and then Travis heard him wander off.

Maggie sighed. "Okay, Deputy, guess I'd better get you home."

Travis tried to roll over and stand, but managed to only come to a sitting position. Around him, the world still spun. He shook his head, hoping to clear it, but that only made it worse.

"You are pretty stupid, you know that?" she chided.

Even through the drunken haze, he agreed with her. He was pretty stupid. And he'd failed. Everything was about ready to come crashing down on top of him. The only consolation was being too damn drunk to give much of a shit.

Something buzzed in his pocket. It buzzed again. For a brief second, he wasn't sure what it was. And then he felt a squirming hand in his pocket and sensed a shape hovering over him.

"Hello?" Maggie said.

And he realized she had retrieved and answered his cell phone.

"No," she said into the phone. "He's with me now, but he is…a…in the middle of something. Yes, he did ask me to answer his phone for him. Can I relay a message?"

Travis tried to reach up for the phone, wanting to answer it himself.

"Uh, huh," Maggie said. "I'll let him know, thanks."

"What…?" Travis managed to say.

"That was that nice lady, Beatrice, back at your office. She told me to tell you that someone named Roy Foster came by looking for you. He said something about Harold Roberson. I'm to tell you that Roy said that Harold's death was not a heart attack at all. He was attacked by an alligator. That club owner, Atticus, has been lying to you all along."

TWENTY SEVEN

TERRITORIAL

WHILE MAGGIE DROVE back to the golf course behind the wheel of his patrol vehicle, Travis did everything he could to sober himself up—sticking his head in the cold, wet air blowing from the air conditioner vents, slapping himself hard on the cheeks, and even shaking his head violently, which almost brought on another wave of nausea. He could still taste the foul acid that had burned his throat raw when he'd shoved a finger down it to make himself sick before climbing into the SUV, hoping to purge some of the alcohol from his system. But nothing was working. He was still very drunk, and this was a sticky sort of drunk, one in which he was more aware of his surroundings than he had any right to be but was unable to do anything about it. If he had been at home, he would have waited it out on the sofa, watching something lame on TV. But he couldn't. Not this time. *Get it together.* He slapped himself again, harder than before.

"You keep doing that you're going to knock your teeth out," Maggie said from the driver's seat.

He wiped drool from the corners of his mouth and nodded back.

"You need to eat something," she said. "It will settle your stomach."

While he wasn't so sure, he realized he hadn't eaten anything the entire night. Perhaps eating something now might help him get back on his feet quicker. He clicked open the armrest storage box. There were a couple of energy bars and a can of warm ice tea inside with the picture of some basketball player on it he didn't recognize.

"Seems now I was right, wasn't I?" she said. "I knew that story about a heart attack was not true. Now that I've seen that it's a crocodile, I am one-hundred percent sure about it. I have to admit, if it were a smaller alligator, then that man being dragged off by it kind of makes sense, but crocodilia are very simple in their thinking. They wouldn't attack something much larger than themselves unless they were threatened by it and had no other choice. There are plenty of birds and fish and other wildlife to feed on deep in the Everglades, so for them to attack a fully grown man makes little sense to me. But that one we saw in the video...? I'm now almost certain that it was just protecting its own territory."

"Territory?" Travis croaked, the initial rumblings of an idea coming to him. It was a crazy idea, one he probably would not have ever come up with sober. But it was there just waiting to be tried.

"Yes, territory. Big crocodiles like that are fiercely territorial. They will protect their turf from any other animal that attempts to invade...their space."

"We didn't see many others in the water," he started to say then shut his eyes and pinched his brow between his fingers to drive away the dizziness.

"Many what?"

"Other gators," he finally managed to say, and then bit into one of the warm energy bars he'd just opened. Chocolate, with nuts. It was hard to choke down that first bite, but he knew if he could he'd feel better for it.

"While you were out hunting...? Hmm. It could be that the big one was in the area, but was avoiding you. Or it could mean a hundred other things."

"Like what?" he said, chewing.

"Lemme see. It could just mean you were unlucky, or were in the wrong spot, or maybe even that you were very lucky and it just didn't know you were there. Or it could have been sleeping, or hunting, or whatever. See? Lots of things."

He peeled down the silver wrapper on the energy bar and prepared to take another bite. "I thought they only hunted at night."

"Not always," she said. "Not always," she repeated, "but sometimes…"

"What?" he said, mouth full.

"It just sounds like it is protecting something," she said. "I can't say what that might be. Maybe Dr. Galen might know more. I'll try his phone again when we stop. I have an idea, though. Want to hear it?"

He swallowed. *Protecting something?* When she had said that, the final parts of his crazy plan had clicked into place. He now knew how they could find it. And he also knew how they could kill it.

TWENTY EIGHT

STOMACH TROUBLES

BY THE TIME they arrived at Clearwater Creek Golf Course, the circus had come to town. The entire parking lot was filled with media trucks of all sizes. Satellite dishes had been deployed, and there were reporters already primping and preening themselves in side mirrors, or testing microphones. White popup tents had been set up on the grassy knoll to the far right of the clubhouse, and the entire area was awash in so many color banners and logos that Travis was now somewhat glad he was still intoxicated. He wasn't at all sure how he was going to handle it all, but for the moment, he really didn't care.

Then he saw the sheriff's cruiser, and swallowed hard. The cruiser was flanked by three other county vehicles. Travis glanced at the radio in his own vehicle and realized he hadn't turned it on the entire way here. Now he was more than a little afraid to do so. But Ms. Scott hadn't said anything about it on the phone to Maggie, so…

"This is not good," Maggie said, "not good at all. Where should I park?"

For a brief moment, he considered telling her to turn around and just drive him home. This was too much to handle right now. No job was worth this much trouble. But, he couldn't do that. It wasn't in him to walk away from anything. They'd have to chase him away like they had in Oregon.

He pointed out a spot to park off to one side. It was not exactly a parking space, so she had to drive up and over a curb to get to it.

She shut off the engine, and with it went the air conditioner. Everything groaned to silence.

He opened his door and the dome light went on, and the dinger inside the dashboard started beeping.

"You sure you are ready for this?" Maggie asked.

"No," he said and stumbled out of the SUV, straightened, and brushed himself off as best he could. He tilted sideways to sniff his uniform, realizing quickly that he stank like the brackish swamp and was still very damp. But there was nothing he could do about it now. He had no spare uniforms waiting for him.

And when he looked back up, three sheriff's deputies were walking in his direction, so it made any thoughts of changing uniforms moot.

"Please come with us," one of the deputies said as the group drew near.

Travis gave a last look at Maggie, tried to grin, and then followed the deputies back to the entrance to the clubhouse. Wordlessly, they led him through the glass front doors, back past the pro shop, and finally through the double doors and into the office of one, Atticus Goulding. Travis's feet sloshed and squished inside his boots the entire way.

In the office, his boss, the county sheriff, was there waiting for him as well. The stern-faced man did not look happy. The sheriff was dressed impeccably in a dark green shirt with a highly polished gold badge, sparkling gold stars on his shoulders, colorful awards and ribbons on his chest, and a black tie held in place by a golden clip. Two shiny gold pens stuck up from his chest pocket, and not a single hair on his well-groomed head was even slightly out of place. This was a man, Travis knew, that was ready to pose and pontificate in front of all those cameras and media hounds just waiting for him outside like expertly conditioned lapdogs. This was a man who reveled in the spotlight. He was also a man looking to find someone he could pretend to support and protect, while at the same time staking that same someone out there like a sacrificial goat for the lions.

Just like my dad, Travis thought.

"Where have you been?" Sheriff Elliot Perez demanded.

Travis came to a stop, straightened, burped into his fist, and said, "Looking for a big alligator."

He could tell from the moment he had walked into the office that it was all over for him. There would be no apologies that would work this time. No excuses that could be made for his terrible behavior. Nothing at all could save him. And, if he were being completely honest, he was quite happy that he was still drunk. He wasn't sure he'd have to courage to face it otherwise. Being fired twice in one year? *My wife is truly a saint if she stays with me this time around.*

He remained at attention as best he could, but he continued to wobble a bit.

Sheriff Perez cleared his throat. "I'm disappointed with you, Deputy Morrison. We have been trying to contact you all morning. You have not answered your radio. We expected you to at least check in with us and update us on your status, and, for a time, we thought something bad might have happened to you. But that doesn't seem to be the case, now, does it?" He cleared his throat then adjusted his cuffs. "I took a great risk in hiring you and now it turns out I may have made a serious mistake in judgment doing so. What do you have to say for yourself?"

Travis wanted to tell the sheriff that the man could have just let Ms. Scott know that he was looking for him. She could have called him on his cellphone. Atticus Goulding had even called him. If the sheriff had been too stupid to figure that out, then…well, that was his problem. He also wanted to let the man know all about how Atticus Goulding had lied about the death of Harold Robertson, and how it had not been a heart attack that had killed the guy. He wanted to tell the sheriff just how Atticus had sought to cover up the fact that it was an alligator attack all along that had killed Mr. Robertson. He wanted to tell him that he'd warned Mr. Goulding several times that the golf course should be closed due to a clear and present danger. He wanted to tell him that he'd been out all night with, supposedly—though the jury was still out on that one—the best alligator hunter in all of Florida. But instead, he had come home empty handed, not even having seen a single sign of the giant crocodile.

He also wanted to mention that he had scientists coming in from Florida Tech to help track down the alligator, or crocodile. And, finally, he had wanted to say that he still recommended closing the entire goddamned course until the alligator—no, the giant *fucking* crocodile—could be located and killed, and that he now had a plan that might just work, crazy at it might be.

But he couldn't do any of this because from the very depths of his stomach came a rumbling roar.

He put a fist over his mouth, hoping it was only a brewing burp. But that rumbling suddenly turned unexpectedly into an explosive spray of vomit that burst forth. Chunks of watery brown goo spewed past his lips and coated the big desk in front of him, splashed all over the pristine sheriff and his men, and speckled the owner of the golf course, still seated in his overstuffed leather chair.

TWENTY NINE

AFTERMATH

"WHAT HAPPENED IN there?" Maggie asked as Travis came to join her over by his former patrol vehicle. He sat on the curb in front of it, bent forward, placed his hands on top of his head, and laced his fingers.

"I've been fired," he said.

"Fired? For what?"

"Don't ask. But I expect I'll be blamed for all this shortly."

"How can they do that? That would be totally unfair."

He shrugged. "Ahh, maybe it's for the best. I just wasn't cut out for this line of work, anyway." He drew a deep breath, let it out. "I'll find something else."

There was a long silence between them. She sat beside him and picked at a nail, then reached down and selected a bit of gravel and flicked it away, and finally sighed before adjusting her glasses and looking at him again.

"What about those poor people who died? Is the sheriff finally going to shut down the golf course?"

"I don't know," he said. "They should. You were right all along. I was just too afraid of losing my job to tell them that. I should have just had the balls to shut it down in the first place and risked unemployment."

"Well, you can go tell the media that now. They are all here. You can spill the entire story and they will have to shut it down."

He sighed. "I was told in no uncertain terms that I'm to vacate the property and say nothing to the media. If I don't leave of my own free will, I will be arrested for obstruction of justice and whatever other charges can be brought against me. Though, when I was told that, the sheriff was not exactly paying much attention to what he was saying. He was a little preoccupied." Travis chuckled, head shaking side to side. "It's just over. You should get the hell out of here before it gets really crazy."

"We came here together in your car."

"Oh...yeah." He drew a breath. "I'll call my wife. She'll come pick us up and give you a ride back to your car."

"Or..." Maggie reached in her pocket and brought out a set of keys. She dangled them in the air and shook them. They jingled.

"I didn't even take them back from you, did I?" Travis asked, bewildered by his thoughtlessness.

It was just one more thing that he'd screwed up, small as it might be. Just one more...

Other than the moment he realized he'd shot some poor kid holding a toy gun back in Oregon, he'd never been so low. Now he faced a bleak future with no job prospects, probably barely enough in the bank for a month or two's living expenses, a son who was probably still pissed off at him, and a wife, who, while supportive, was more likely closer to a breaking point than she was letting on.

His father had been right about him all along. He sighed again. He was not cut out for a career in law enforcement. He didn't have what it took to be part of that thin blue line between order and chaos. Those men and women were the real heroes. He was just a loser and always had been a loser.

And he'd just lost again.

"Let's go," he said, stood, and adjusted what remained of his uniform after his badge had been removed, leaving a ripped patch of cloth where it had once been. Fortunately, none of his own vomit had landed on him even though he had caused a real mess in that office. Oddly, and though he knew he shouldn't be feeling this way, he was experiencing a certain level of joy and satisfaction over what he'd left behind in there.

"What about the sheriff? Will they come after us?"

"He's going to be busy with the press soon. I doubt he will notice us for a while, and, by then, we can leave the damn thing parked outside the station. I'm sure Ms. Scott can arrange for them to pick it up."

THIRTY

NESTING

"THEY TOOK YOUR gun?" Maggie asked from behind the wheel as she drove the SUV.

"Yeah. Badge, too." He shrugged, patting the spot on his shirt where it had been, and tucking the torn cloth inside and against his white, but not so white now, T-shirt.

"That sucks."

"I'll figure it out."

"Again," she said. "I can't get the image of that attack out of my mind. It just…haunts me, you know? It would have been so easy to prevent it, too."

He did know. For the past hour though, he'd been focused on his own survival. While it had not been a life and death struggle in Atticus's office, it had been difficult to process all the blooming implications of now being unemployed, sacked—fired.

But her out of the blue mention of the man trying to save his son triggered it again in his mind and brought all the horrors back, causing him to wonder if he was focusing on what was truly important. *That man died. Needlessly. To save his son. The ultimate price to pay.* And then he suddenly became very worried that if they went ahead with the tournament, it would lead to another disaster. That sheriff didn't seem prepared to do anything about it, either.

How many more have to die because I failed to act...?

He grunted. "You said those things are territorial, right?"

"Yes," she replied, taking a turn onto a single lane blacktop road that would take them back to the boat dock. "Very territorial."

"How big are their territories, generally?"

She thought about it for a moment, drumming her hands on the wheel. "Depends on the relative size of the crocodilia and what they are protecting. Mostly they attack to protect their hunting grounds. Or where they have stashed prey underwater. Or, sometimes where they nest."

Travis pulled at his jaw and released it. "Ely said that thing was female."

"I don't know how he could tell for sure," she said. "There was no way I could tell from the video."

"What if it was female?" Travis asked. "And what if it was indeed protecting something important to it?"

"Like a nest?" she said.

"Exactly. That's what I've been thinking."

"Well, I suppose that it could be protecting its nest. It might make sense, given the displayed behavior."

He nodded. "Since we never saw it the other night, we were never close enough to that nest. We mostly stayed in one place."

"And it never showed," she added.

"Yup," he said, nodding. The part of his plan that had started to take hold earlier became more of a nagging need. It made sense now. It made perfect sense.

"What if we found that nest?" he asked. "What then?"

She hesitated for a beat, then replied, "It would do anything it could to protect it."

THIRTY ONE

WHY THE HELL NOT?

THE SUN WAS high in the sky when they arrived at the boat launch. Still parked under the shade of an enormous mangrove tree was an old rusting pickup truck with a white door that didn't match whatever color paint was on the rest of the truck.

Ely Beauregard Stone.

Travis could see the old guy was sleeping sideways across the bench seat as he approached. Both doors hung open, and Ely wore a tattered baseball cap pulled down to cover his face, which he didn't even bother to remove as Travis approached.

"What? You back?" Ely said from under the hat, not moving an inch.

"I got fired," Travis said.

Ely removed the hat and pulled himself up by the steering wheel. He grinned wryly, showing a gap where his canine tooth should have been. He probed the gap with his tongue and then licked his lips.

"Well, well. What fer?"

"That isn't important. Can you take us back out there?"

"Out there? Who'm I takin'?"

"Me and the marine biologist I told you about."

Ely leaned sideways and stared as Travis followed his gaze. Maggie waved back from behind him and stepped closer to the truck.

"He has a plan. I think it might work."

"Plan, eh? No one really hunts gators during the day, son, but come back tonight. I'll take you out so's we can kill some more gators. Or you can go a swimmin' with 'em again if ya'd like. Jus' don't go drinking so much."

Travis ignored the joke. "I no longer have the authority to let you kill any alligators that you find now. I'm just a private citizen. Got fired."

"Ya did, huh?" He kept chuckling, then stopped. "Pay it no never mind. Not that I followed them laws much anyway. What's yer plan and who's payin'?" He glanced from Travis to Maggie, then gave her a leering wink.

Travis frowned. "If we catch this giant gator, you will become a legend."

Ely cackled and pulled himself out of his seat and to his feet. He stretched his skinny arms, yawned, rolled his shoulders, then began to scratch himself under his right armpit. "Already am a legend, sonny."

"Then do it for bragging rights?"

"Who'm I gonna brag to?"

Travis exhaled heavily. With each new refusal, he grew a bit more insistent and determined inside. He knew his plan was a crazy one, but it was drop-dead simple. And simple plans usually worked the best. If he pulled this off, he might even get his old job back. That was, if he wanted it back. Or, even better, he might keep some other father from suffering the same terrible fate of the one who had died trying to save his son.

"Take us out, okay? We'll work out any payments later. Right now, we need to find that monster before it can kill again."

Ely snorted and spat. "None of them folks believed you 'bout it did they?"

"Nope," Travis said. "So, can you take us out on your boat?"

Ely squinted while his mouth moved as if he were chewing on something. He reached up to pick his teeth, then spat.

"Sure," he said, "why the hell not?"

THIRTY TWO

SEDATE IT

UNDER THE BLISTERING Florida sun, the boat puttered its way down a thin channel cut between two sandy banks bursting with chaotic growth. Ely seemed to know the way, even though Travis had no idea where that way led to at the moment. He had simply given the old man a final destination, and Ely raised one eyebrow, winked, and said it would not be a problem getting there.

Maggie sat in the back of the boat this time, working on some equipment she'd brought along. She'd complained that she needed a few other things that she'd left behind at Florida Tech, but that was over five hours away by car. It was five hours they didn't have. Travis wondered then if he had much time at all. With all those pesky news media people onsite at the golf course, some of them were bound to wander into places where they shouldn't. And with no one there to actively prevent another attack...?

Granted, they were only representatives of the news media, and though he might hold out disdain for their work in general, that didn't mean he wanted to see any of them dead. Well, maybe some. Those same vicious groups of bottom feeders that had hammered the stories about him over and over on the six o'clock news, saying how he'd had malicious intent when he'd shot and killed that poor dumb kid with the fake gun, which couldn't be further from the truth. That moment he had shot the kid had only been a brief instance in time. Too short, really. He had simply reacted as he had been trained to do and made a dreadful mistake. He would pay the steep price for it the rest of his life because there was no taking it back.

Not ever.

"How far?" he asked. One channel was beginning to look like any other. It was a regular maze, and how Ely knew his way around, Travis had no idea.

"Give-ur-take 'bout ten minutes," Ely said from behind the wheel. He stood with one foot propped up on the side of the boat. A long trail of blue exhaust smoke trailed out behind them, hovering just over the surface of the dark water.

Travis shifted nearer to the coolers that he'd come across earlier. One held fish heads for bait, another held the dynamite. Enough dynamite, he hoped, to blow that damn monster into tiny meaty chunks. He sucked a drink from a bottle of water, wiped his brow, and cracked open the cooler with the dynamite in it.

The cooler was empty.

He turned and gave a questioning look at Ely.

The skinny gray-bearded man chuckled and reached down under the podium with the steering wheel on it. He came back with a bundle of dynamite wrapped with duct tape and sporting a foot long green fuse.

"Thought of it myself," Ely said, giving a sharp wink and a head nod. "We find that thing, we blow it straight to hell. Eh?"

"What are you talking about?" Maggie said. "I thought we planned to sedate it. I even brought—"

"Sedate it?" Ely said, incredulously. "How ya planning to do that?"

"With this." She held up a long silver pole.

"Missy, that's not going to take out no gator. Betted to shoot it, 'er blow it up."

"I've quad dosed these darts with Azaperone. This is enough to take down a fully grown bull elephant. Plenty, maybe more than enough for a crocodile of that size." She held up a long cylindrical dart with red fletchings on one end.

Ely scoffed and spat over the side of the boat. "That'll just piss it off. Use that n'stead." He pointed with a nod at his crossbow rig that was resting against the side rail to his left. "Put a nice big hole in her side and she'll bleed out quick."

"I'm not here to kill it," she said.

Travis cleared his throat. "Supposing that you do manage to sedate it. What then?"

"We can tie it up and drag it ashore," she said as if the solution were obvious. "I will keep it sedated until Dr. Galen arrives. Then we can decide what to do with it."

Travis nodded. It was no use arguing with her. If she thought she could sedate it, then good. That would make it easier for him to blow it the hell up.

THIRTY THREE

SCARS

ELY CUT THE throttle and the motor dropped to an idle. Travis was standing and scanning the way ahead. The marshland was too entangled with overgrowth to be certain, but he was sure he'd seen the lush greenness of the golf course in the far distance as they'd approached, so he was certain they were now nearing his desired destination.

"I don't see any signs it came through here," Maggie said. "With something that big, there'd probably be some bent vegetation—or something. Footprints on the banks, whatever."

Ely chuckled. "Where the hell you learn that? Gators don't leave no big signs to track 'em."

"They should," she said.

"Missy, you ever done this before? You ever tracked gator through a swamp?"

"I've been on swamp walks before. I know what I'm looking for."

"You sure about that?"

"Yes, I'm sure," she said. "How about you?"

"Missy, I've been huntin' gators since I was as high as my dadda's pecker." He set one foot up on the bench and lifted his ragged shirt.

Ely's skin was pasty white and sickly looking under his threadbare shirt, but there were ragged marks along his abdomen in the shape of a horseshoe.

"One got me when I was 'bout ten. Damn near dragged me off. Kilt 'em with my bare hands, I did. You? You ever been bitten by a gator?"

"No," she said sharply and glanced back at Travis.

He shrugged. Other than breaking an arm falling off a motorcycle, he'd never been seriously injured. And it wasn't as if there was some big need to go comparing scars right now. That would be silly.

Ely let his shirt down. "So, Missy, you don't go telling me I ain't know what I'm doing."

She seemed to seethe for a moment. Then she said, "I don't appreciate you calling me 'Missy.'" She returned to the duffle bag she'd set in the back of the boat. She unzipped it and brought out the .44 Magnum and began to strap the belt around her waist.

"Whoa," Ely said. "Now that's a gun. Okay, won't be calling ya no more 'Missy.' But, girl, so's you know, Missy was my daughter, God rest her soul. Weren't no insult to ya. You jus' reminded me of her, is all."

Maggie stared at Travis for a moment. He could see a change come over her as she seemed to be reassessing a number of things. She blinked and then wiped at the corner of her eye and hefted the gun, and instead of strapping it to her waist, she held it out for him to take.

He didn't take it right away, so she jiggled the gun. "You can back me up with it, that's all. But, please, whatever you do, don't shoot the crocodile."

He neither nodded nor shook his head. He just smiled a little. Since he'd had to give up his gun and his badge, he felt a little naked and unprepared for what they were doing. His overall plan was still the same, but now that he had a gun to fall back on, things seemed a tiny bit better.

"There's more ammo if you need it. But not much." She indicated toward the bag. "You do know how to shoot one of these, don't you?"

THIRTY FOUR

OFF BALANCE

"IF SHE HAS a nest anywhere, it'd probably be over on that sandbar," Maggie said.

Travis was using an old wooden paddle to move the boat while Ely sat up on the bow, foot propped up on the side, saying nothing, but watching the water closely.

"What's a nest look like?" Travis asked.

"With crocodiles, they will usually dig a hole and lay their eggs in it. Though, some make mounds."

"How many eggs?"

"Sixty…maybe eighty total."

"Eighty? You mean there could be eighty more of those things?"

"No, usually only a few survive to adulthood. Most are eaten by birds or snakes or even other crocodilia."

"What about male crocodiles?" he asked. "How did this thing breed?"

She shrugged. "It is impossible to tell for sure. We are dealing with something that has never been seen before. We'll know more when we can capture it and study it further."

He nodded back and his hand let go of the oar and instinctively crept to the large handgun on his side.

The boat jerked forward as the bow end scraped against the bank. Maggie came forward with a long metal stick she'd called a "boomstick" that was now loaded with the tranquilizer dart. She leapt off the boat and sank to her knees as she slipped and slid on the muddy bank.

"Not a good idea to go stomping around up there," Ely said.

"I know what I'm doing," she replied.

Ely raised the crossbow from where he had stashed it beside himself and set it across his lap.

She pushed her way up the bank and into the bushes. Travis stood and joined Ely as he watched her disappear into the dense overgrowth up from the beach.

"You sure she should be doing this?" he asked.

"She shouldn't," Ely said. "Not alone."

Shutting his eyes, then opening them, Travis made a decision, hoping it wasn't going to prove to be his last. He stepped over the side of the boat and splashed to the shore. "I'm going with her," he stated, in part to screw up his own courage.

He sucked in a deep breath and plunged into the entangled vegetation.

"Hey," he said in a whispered shout.

Nothing.

"Hey, where are you?" he said a little louder.

He spun to look behind him and the tall reeds closed in around him. He heard nothing but buzzing insects. Saw nothing but thin vertical shapes. He swallowed hard and his heart started pulsing heavily in his throat.

"This was a bad idea," he whispered to himself.

Then he heard a sound. He spun, reaching for the big gun at his side—

"Hey, yourself," Maggie whispered. "I found something. Keep quiet, okay?"

He sighed out a held breath and nodded. His fear was almost palpable, and he was regretting his decision to embark on this foolish endeavor. Not if that giant crocodile could be nearby. All he could think of now was making his way back to the safety of the boat.

But she was obviously not thinking the same thing. She led him through the tall grasses and to the other side of what turned out to be a small island. On the opposite bank, the vegetation was significantly shorter, and he could see the dark waters beyond. There was another sandbar visible, just across the channel, but to get to it, they would need to wade into the dark waters first. He had no idea how deep it was in the middle. *Two feet? Ten feet?*

"That could be what we are looking for over there," she said. "See that open stretch of beach? That's a perfect spot for a nest."

"You first," he said.

She grinned back and raised the boomstick, head twisting left and right. Took a tentative step forward and her boot sank in the water, and she wobbled sideways, but regained her balance and took another awkward step. He followed, mud sucking at his boots as each off-balance step through the murky waters brought on even more fear, driving him closer and closer to the edge of complete panic.

But he knew he couldn't succumb to panic. She was doing fine, so he didn't want her to think he was as afraid of all this as he was. He waded forward another step.

And—

There was a loud boom. A human cry of surprise. Birds shot from the bushes, racing for the sky. Another deep booming noise came from behind, the sound of metal on metal.

"Ely," Maggie breathed.

THIRTY FIVE

TWANG

TRAVIS HAD THE .44 Magnum out in an instant and was splashing through the water in the direction he had heard the terrible sounds. Maggie was right on his heels. Even though he had been filled with fear just a few seconds ago, he was able to quickly push that fear aside and let his training and instincts take over.

Bursting through the reedy grasses on the side of the small island where they had landed, he saw the flat-bottomed boat about twenty yards off to his left. It had overturned completely. The engine and propeller were now stuck up in the air.

And a few yards past the boat he saw it—the croc, the gator, the...

The scale of the whole thing shocked him. Seeing it for real and not just in a tiny video clip sent shivers racing up and down his spine. *Jesus...* It was just...huge. The scale seemed off the charts, like he was not seeing angles and distances correctly. The thing was bigger than the boat by ten feet at least. *Huge*, was all he could think. And it was now working its way around to one side of the overturned boat, but it also became clear that one of its front legs had snagged on something. It stopped and started thrashing back and forth, attempting to free itself from its entanglement.

Travis raised the handgun to fire.

"No!" Maggie yelled from beside him, hand going up in warning. She rushed forward, going directly for the large creature with the boomstick with the tranquilizer dart in it raised like a spear. She intended to stab it as soon as she was close enough.

Because she was now in front of him, he had no clear line of fire at it. He shifted sideways and backed up onto the bank and sprinted after her, leaping over tangled roots at the water's edge, pounding his boots deep into the sandy soil.

As she closed with the thing, she raised the metal stick and was seeking to bring it down directly behind the crocodile's front leg and prod it in the side there, which Travis remembered being a position of vulnerability.

But she missed when the giant beast drew itself away and slithered backward into the water. She stumbled after it, going into the water up to her hips as she gave chase. But it continued to draw away from her, deeper, ever deeper.

That was when he saw that the boat was being pulled sideways and steadily toward the water. It was dredging sand and catching on roots as it went—and finally it stopped completely. He saw a flash of light and realized what had caused it. There was a cable attaching the crocodile to the boat, and that line was now drawn as taut as a guitar string.

The boat continued to pull away from the shore but caught on something and tipped up, burying the bow end and raising the engine high in the air. What had once been inside the boat clattered and created a great cacophony of crashing metal and fiberglass and wood as whatever hadn't been strapped down dumped out at the water's edge.

The plastic cooler so important to his plan also spilled out and bobbed in the water next to the nearly upright and vertical hull. He ran toward the cooler, then he remembered that the dynamite he sought was no longer in it. Ely had taken it out and had set it under the steering podium. He readjusted and ran to the boat, ever wary of the giant crocodile backing away. The huge thing sank into the water and finally dropped under the surface and appeared now like a giant floating island, moving away slowly.

Then it completely submerged.

Maggie came to a halt, boomstick still raised like a spear. She was glancing all around her and backing away, coming closer and closer to the shore as if in reverse.

The boat continued to shift and move and turn upward, threatening to tumble completely over and land on him. The bow end remained caught on something and the entire boat bounced and shuddered and rattled in the air.

Then there was suddenly another flash and a loud *twang* as the wire that had tethered the crocodile to the boat snapped and the loose end whipped at the water. The boat stayed upright for a brief few seconds, then came crashing down, raising a white spray, blinding him as he closed in on the boat, and soaking him in the foul, brackish water.

Spitting away bits of mud he had nearly inhaled, he shoved his way forward. When he reached the boat, he crabbed sideways and ducked low to get to the steering podium, trying to locate the dynamite.

It was not there.

He ducked out from under the hull and scanned the area around him, picking through the floating debris. He smelled gasoline and saw an oily rainbow slick as the red gas can bobbed away from the boat.

A cry came from the opposite side of the hull.

But it wasn't just a cry. It was the sound of someone swearing and cursing in anger. Travis rounded the boat and found Ely lying sideways on the embankment. One of the old man's legs was bent nearly around, and the foot was pointing in a very unnatural direction. Ely was gripping his leg and wincing in pain while scooting himself away from the water's edge. The fired crossbow was about ten feet away from him. Travis ran to it and picked it up. The quiver was missing. He scanned for it, but did not see it anywhere.

"Put two bolts in 'em," Ely said through gritted teeth. "It's bleeding now, but not enough. Thought I could wire it to the boat."

Ely then went back to swearing and cursing, which Travis ignored as he got down on one knee to examine Ely's leg. A broken leg seemed to be the only thing wrong with the man. He rose to his feet when Maggie came up alongside him.

"It's going to come back," she said. "We better get ready for it."

And the split-second she had finished saying that, the water churned and frothed and a blur of movement and noise and confusion knocked Travis from his feet. Something bumped him, hard, sending him cartwheeling through the air. He was tossed about like a rag doll and it seemed to take forever before he landed. But land, he did. Hard. He rolled and rolled then came to a stop flat on his back and surrounded by grass too tall to see past.

THIRTY SIX

FIRE AND FLAMES

LAYING THERE FLAT on his back, Travis questioned his own sanity. Here he was in the middle of a swamp doing battle with a giant crocodile. He laughed and that laughter grew louder. But then it came to a screeching halt when his mind returned to the seriousness of the situation.

Maybe I am a bit mad...? Maybe this was a truly and utterly stupid idea.

But he was here now. He had the .44 Magnum still. He sat up and pulled the revolver out of the holster and flipped open and spun the cylinder—six shiny bullets, all unfired. He snapped it shut. He didn't quite know why he had done that. It was completely unnecessary to check that the gun was loaded. But it just felt right to do so.

He was in pain and when he sucked in air, it hurt. *Broken rib, probably.* But he wasn't going to let that stop him. He pushed himself over onto all fours, then slowly rose to his feet and stumbled back to the boat.

As he entered the clearing, he reassessed the scene. Ely was missing. Maggie was at the water's edge.

"It got him," she said matter of factly. "That damn thing just came up on shore and got him. I-I couldn't stop it."

She held up the boomstick. "It didn't work. I tried, but the armor on its back was just too thick. The needle couldn't even penetrate. It bent."

"That's okay," Travis said. He put a hand on her shoulder.

Ely was a crazy old coot, but Travis felt a great loss now that the man was gone. He sighed. It would be difficult to—

The water frothed and the giant crocodile surfaced again. He snapped up the .44 Magnum right as the big thing rolled over onto its side. He fired. The gun's report was deafening and he could barely control the recoil. As his arm dropped back onto target, he fired again, and again. He wasn't sure if any of the bullets had hit the beast, but he was fairly certain some had.

Along the crocodile's side, an arrow stuck out, still trailing the metal wire that had tied it to the boat. That wire had wrapped around one of its legs, pinning it. As the creature came back up, Travis froze.

Ely was trapped in the crocodile's enormous jaws. All that was visible though was Ely's torso. The rest of the man was inside the thing, clamped between its teeth. Ely was bleeding from his mouth, but was miraculously still alive. One of his hands was shaped in a fist and was beating on the crocodile's head, as if he was attempting to make it release him.

And in his other hand...

Travis ran to the water's edge, raising the .44 Magnum, looking for a vulnerable spot to shoot. Even the big .44 would have trouble penetrating the animal's thick scales along its back, especially at such an awkward angle. Travis would just have to get closer.

Ely was trying to say something. The crocodile settled for a brief second. Travis shook his head, trying to process what the old man had said. His ears still rang from the gun's report. He waded deeper into the water.

Then what the man had been trying to say suddenly made sense.

Travis shoved one hand in his pocket. He came back with the cigarette lighter he had taken from his son and had kept with him ever since, absentmindedly transferring it from pocket to pocket as he changed uniforms. He flicked it. Flicked it again. It caught. He extended an arm, lowering the flickering flame to the water and closer to the rainbow sheen.

The tiny flame ignited the gasoline and oil floating on the water with a *whoosh*. A great fire bloomed and he backpedaled away from it and up onto to the sandy bank. Maggie was alongside him in an instant, and together they watched as the flames made their way out and into deeper water, growing closer and closer to the giant crocodile.

Ely, hand clutching the bundled dynamite, continued to pound away on the crocodile's jaw. He had seen the flames and was waiting for them to get closer to him.

Travis could see it clearly. The flames would reach Ely and the old man would dip his arm closer to the water's surface and light the fuse on the dynamite, then blow himself and the giant crocodile straight to Hell. He didn't want the old guy to die, but there was nothing that could be done about it now. Positions reversed, he'd want to go out the same way.

The old man was about to be a hero, and that damn beast was about to be blown into chunks of flesh.

But the moment before the flames reached Ely, the old man fell limp.

"No," Travis mumbled. "No...this can't be."

Ely slumped further, and before the flames could reach the fuse, the dynamite in his hand sank beneath the surface of the water.

THIRTY SEVEN

DEFLATED

TRAVIS RAISED THE .44 Magnum and fired the remaining rounds at the crocodile. But they did nothing. Like he had thought, they ricocheted harmlessly off the thing's heavy armor as it sank low in the water.

He lowered the empty weapon, watching as the crocodile descended beneath the surface.

"Poor Ely," Maggie said.

Travis said nothing. He closed his eyes and lowered his head. *Lord, take this man into Your waiting arms.* It had always been his belief that when one died they went to a better place. One day he would go to that place and he hoped to meet Ely there and perhaps share a drink with the old guy.

He opened his eyes.

In front of him was the quiver that had once been attached to the crossbow. It bobbed in the water in the tiny waves next to shore. He bent to pick it up. On it was a single remaining crossbow bolt.

Maybe, he thought. *Just maybe.*

"Let's go," he said.

Maggie waited beside him, leaning heavily on the long aluminum boomstick. "Where?"

"Follow me."

He stopped to retrieve the crossbow and reloaded it, then set off across the small island.

They emerged on the opposite side.

"What are you doing?" Maggie asked.

He said nothing.

"We should leave," she said. "We can always come back. It's too dangerous to remain here."

He again said nothing. He waded into the water. It kept getting deeper and deeper.

"Stop," she finally said as he was halfway across to the sandbar they had spotted earlier. "If you go there, it will certainly attack."

"Good," he said and kept marching. He was planning on it.

The sucking mud and water grew deeper until it was up to his chin, then once again ramped up the other way and became shallow. He trudged forward onto the sandbar. She joined him, also dripping wet.

"You think the nest is here, right?"

"It should be."

"Find it," he said, moving into a guarding position higher on the bank.

She kicked sand with her foot and moved in a widening circle. He watched her and he watched the water for any signs the crocodile might be approaching. Ripples, movement, anything.

Nothing.

She stopped. She kicked the sand again with her toe of one boot. And again.

"Here it is," she said.

He joined her and they dug the sand away with their fingers until the hints of white eggs became visible. The eggs were not at all what he expected. They were each about the size of a baseball.

"We shouldn't be here," she said. "We should leave this alone. They aren't due to hatch for weeks."

He ignored her and grabbed an egg from the nest. He wound up like a pitcher and threw the egg as hard as he could. It sailed in an arc and landed somewhere on the other island.

"What the hell are you doing?" she asked. "You can't do that!" She stepped away from him, turning her back on the water.

He didn't care about the eggs. He only cared that he was destroying the spawn of that monster. Some things were just far too dangerous to let live.

He grabbed another and hurled it. Then another. Finally, he fell into a frenzy, grabbing eggs and throwing them into the water one after another until he could find no more to throw and would have to dig further into the nest.

"That's horrible," she said. "You are killing them all!"

He stopped when he saw the ripples in the water he had made interrupted by a moving shape.

"Get out of my way," he growled.

She must have realized her mistake the second he had said that. Her eyes went suddenly wide and she started to turn to look back at the water. When she had turned far enough, she lunged forward, bolting up the bank in flight, feet kicking sand and mud.

The crocodile shot forth from the water, coming at her with its jaws wide open. Travis could see the rows and rows of dagger-like teeth set in its thick gums. There was still blood and bits of flesh and cloth on those teeth.

Maggie ran away from it, stepping left, then right, making a zig-zag pattern in the sand. Still, it came at her but was moving in a straight line. Its jaws closed and opened and it came to a stop, half in and half out of the water. It started to turn slowly toward Travis, realizing he was closer to the nest it was attempting to protect.

He snatched up the crossbow from the dark sand beside him and raised the weapon to his shoulder, searching for the vulnerable spot Ely had told him about behind the front leg. He lined up on the bent limb and slightly back from the joint and squeezed the trigger.

The crossbow released its bolt in near silence, and the razor-sharp broadhead tip traveled the distance from him to the crocodile in less than the blink of an eye. The bolt thumped as it buried itself deep into the side of the creature.

Instantly, blood began to stream from the new hole. The crocodile opened its jaws again and thrashed back and forth. Blood filled the spraying and churning water around it as it attempted to back away. But it had beached itself too far up and the wire entangling one of its front legs caused that leg to bend outward.

The giant crocodile fell flat on its belly. It tried to push itself back into the water with its entangled leg. Travis ran directly at it, approaching from the side. He had no more crossbow bolts, no more bullets, but he took the butt of the crossbow and began smashing it against the thing's head. He hit it in the eye and that eye burst open. The thing tried to pull back, but it couldn't. It kept moving slower. He ran around to the other side and smashed out its other eye. Then he jumped to the side and tried to leap on top of it, but fell off and onto his ass. He got up and tried again. This time, he climbed up on its head and began pounding the butt of the crossbow down hard on its head. It was like hammering against concrete, but he didn't care. He kept at it over and over. The crocodile moved slower and slower.

Finally—it stopped moving altogether, and it sank heavily to the sandy, debris-filled beach like a deflating balloon. Travis kept pounding until there was no more movement from it. None at all.

Panting, ignoring the ache in his side, he rolled off it and onto the shore, half in and half out of the water.

THIRTY EIGHT

TOO DANGEROUS

TRAVIS PULLED AT the oar and then shifted to the other side of the half-wrecked boat and paddled there too. The boat lazily made its way across the stilled water. He was certain now that they were moving in the right direction. He had seen the golf course in the distance and was keeping his bearings through the trees draped with hanging moss by noting the position of the scorching sun through the branches.

Maggie was using the aluminum pole that had once contained the useless tranquilizer dart to push off the various trees and stumps and make certain they did not become stuck or lose momentum.

"I was wrong," she said somberly.

Travis nodded as he switched sides again to keep the boat from turning. Right or wrong didn't matter any longer. He was still alive. She was alive. And it was dead. That's what truly mattered.

But he also felt a certain kind of sadness. The crocodile was only acting in its own nature. It was protecting its offspring like any good parent would. It was the way of the world, really. He also couldn't let himself be overly troubled by it. Sometimes things were just too dangerous to let live. He knew that now more than ever.

"You weren't wrong," he said. "I don't feel good about killing it, but it had to be done."

"Yeah." She nodded. "I guess you are right."

"I know," he said, trying to lighten the sour mood. "Science. I get it."

But she didn't bite. "No, it's not just that. It had as much right to live as we do."

"Did it?" he asked. "Did it really?"

She said nothing.

"Where do you think that thing came from?" he asked.

She remained silent for several seconds, then, "I don't know. Freak of nature? Evolution? There are more things in Heaven and Earth..."

"...Than are dreamt of in your philosophy," Travis finished. "Yeah, I saw that on TV once. Beer commercial, I think. Or maybe Star Trek."

She chuckled softly. "What do you plan to do now?"

"I plan," he started to say, then shifted to the other side of the boat and pulled on the oar there, "to go home, shower, make love to my wife, and get up tomorrow and pack. We are getting the hell out of this state."

She laughed again.

"You?" he asked.

"We'll come back and study that thing. See if we can figure out where it came from. This could be the find that starts my career. I don't know if you understand this, but being a marine biologist is a difficult job."

"Difficult how?"

"You know the woman or guy with the whistle at Sea World? The one who trains the killer whales?"

"Yeah...?"

"That person is usually a marine biologist like me."

"Makes sense."

"What you probably don't know is that trainer is often a volunteer."

"So the pay sucks, huh?"

"It's terrible," she said.

Travis thought about it for a moment and chuckled to himself. Being a marine biologist was never something he could see himself doing, but he had gained quite a bit of respect for Maggie. He wished her well on wherever her career took her. And as he thought about her career, he wondered what the hell he would do about his. He was done with law enforcement. That was a given. His father had pushed him into it and then had berated him ever since, going so far as to blame him for making that terrible mistake and shooting that poor kid.

But he was done with all that. He would choose what he would do with the rest of his life. Perhaps he could try plumbing, or carpentry, or something that didn't involve so much danger. All he ever wanted was a peaceful life with his wife and son at his side. If all his future thrills and excitement came from watching television and movies, or reading books, then he was okay with that.

Damn straight, he was okay with that.

"One thing I haven't really figured out, though," he started to say.

"What?" she asked with interest.

He thought back on Ely the gator hunter. Pictured the man sitting on his front porch swing and sipping whiskey. It was a glorious sight. So simple. So peaceful a life. Except for the hunting part.

He smiled to himself again and adopted the old hunter's manner of speaking. "If that were the mama gator, where's ya thinks the papa gator?"

THIRTY NINE

EPILOGUE

CLEARWATER CREEK, FLORIDA (Star News Network) - A father and son golf tournament turned into a major bloodbath on Saturday when a giant alligator was spotted attacking golfers as they attempted to flee the course.

Among the dead are Hollywood actors Leonardo Gibson, Jackson Clooney, Tommy Pitts, and Jules Roberts. Also killed were rappers Little Gawayne, Kanye East, and Tick-Tock, along with country singer Twang Heart. Former congressman Buster Clinton and Senator Willy Johnson were also among the dead. Sixteen others suffered injuries including five children, but all are expected to make speedy recoveries.

"It was terrible," said one witness. "That monster just came out of nowhere and started eating people. All those famous stars. Such a tragedy. I don't know how the world is ever going to be the same again."

The man in charge of the event, Atticus Goulding, owner of Clearwater Creek Golf Course, and Sheriff Elliot Perez, tasked with providing security, are expected to be indicted on state and federal charges of fraud, conspiracy, and filing false statements under the Federal Wildlife Act. Additional charges of manslaughter may also be applied, said State Attorney General, Ron Coldbern.

The alligator in question has not been located, but an intense hunt is on to track it down and capture it before it can harm anyone else. Local residents are advised to keep a sharp lookout and make sure that all pets remain indoors. They are also being advised to be diligent for any large reptiles that may seek to enter their property. Preliminary results of the search are expected shortly during a joint press conference with Florida Fish and Wildlife, and the director of Homeland Security, Conner Franks.

Florida Tech Marine Biology Department's Dr. Anthony Galen and research assistant, Maggie Fisk, were in the area at the time of the attack. They had been called in to investigate various alligator habitats when the attack took place. Ms. Fisk reported witnessing earlier attacks by what she claims might have been an extinct species of crocodile (*Sarcosuchus Imperator*, or giant crocodile). She, along with Former Deputy Travis Morrison of the Okatee Sheriff's Department, had earlier attempted to warn both Sheriff Perez and Mr. Goulding of the extreme danger presented by such an animal. They had subsequently advised a complete shutdown of the tournament but were unsuccessful in their efforts. Soon after their failed attempt, Deputy Travis Morrison was terminated for unknown reasons. Deputy Morrison could not be reached for comment.

THE END

Made in the USA
Lexington, KY
05 January 2017